LEANA

JACLYN WEIST

Dragons & Fairy Tales Press

This is a work of fiction, and the views expressed herein are the sole responsibility of the author. Likewise, characters, places, and incidents are either the product of the author's imagination or are represented fictitiously, and any resemblance to actual persons, living or dead, or actual events or locales, is entirely coincidental.

Leana

Book design and layout copyright © 2016 by Dragons & Fairy Tales Press

Cover design copyright © 2016 by Rachelle Hearn

ISBN: 978-1-944137-13-7

Dedication

For Rachelle

Acknowledgments

This book has been a long time coming, and I'm so excited to share it with you. Back when I wrote *Best of Luck,* I discovered the Leanan Sidhe and I've been obsessed with her ever since. She's a pretty awful creature, and I wanted to give her a chance to redeem herself.

I want to thank Lindzee Armstrong and Tristi Pinkston for telling me that I shouldn't stop writing stories based on Celtic mythology because it's who I am. It's what I enjoy. You made me do the brave thing and write this story.

Thank you to my brainstorming friends at the latest writing retreat for helping me figure out the best way to make this story happen.

Thank you to my awesome beta readers for helping me polish the story and make it so much better.

And, of course, thank you to my amazing family for your support. Love you all!

CHAPTER ONE

LEANA

Leana stood and left the lake, already forgetting about the man she'd drained of life moments before. He had been kind, and his music rivaled that of some of the best musicians in the history of Ireland. But he had served his purpose, and it was time to move on.

Her thick red hair blew into her face from the winds of the oncoming storm. It was time to go back to the barrows. If she stayed too long, people would begin to question.

His final moments flashed through her mind, begging for her to help him. But he was already beyond help by that point. The moment he had agreed to court her, he had sealed his fate. The thought made Leana pause, something that had never happened before. He was among countless others that she'd drained, and yet it was the first time she'd almost felt . . . regret.

She squared her shoulders and pushed away the strange human emotion. She was the Leanan Sidhe. It was her duty to provide the inspiration for music, art, and literature that would be remembered for years to come. She had done it for centuries, and would for centuries more.

"Leana? Is that you?" The old woman stood at the doorway. "Come in, or you'll catch your death of cold."

Leana put her arm around the old woman and guided her back into the barrow. "'Tis you I worry about, Mam."

Because of who she was, Leana had to move often so that angry villagers couldn't find her. When she chose this home, it was already occupied. Leana knew that Fiona didn't have much time left on this earth and her memory was poor, so Leana had come as Fiona's long-lost daughter.

"Did you find what you were looking for, dearie?" Fiona dished out some stew and set it on the table in front of Leana.

"Yes, I did, thank you." Leana took a bite, even though she didn't need the nourishment. If Fiona suspected anything, Leana would be forced to leave, and this part of the country was rich in young artists trying to make their way in the world. "This stew is wonderful."

Fiona beamed. "Oh, I am so glad. I will be going to the market tomorrow. Would you like to come with me?"

Leana hesitated. She detested being around humans for long periods of time, but now that the young man was gone, she'd need someone new to feed on. "All right. I may leave early if the storms come in."

"Of, course, dearie." Fiona slumped over on her chair. She'd fallen asleep again.

Leana frowned in disgust. Humans. They were so weak. She still had her beauty after centuries while humans only had theirs for a few decades. It was said that if she didn't feed on the souls of artists, she would also fade and grow old, but Leana wasn't about to test the theory.

She led Fiona into her bed and pulled the covers up, allowing the woman to have comfort for the few days she had left. In three days she would leave the earth and Leana would be alone. It was strange to feel responsible for a human, but then no other human had ever cared for her when they weren't under her spell.

Leana grew impatient as Fiona stopped again in the middle of the trail, trying to catch her breath. Leana had offered to pull the cart, but Fiona insisted on doing it herself. She swore that it kept her young, which was obviously not the case.

The market was loud, and young children ran through the street. Leana's skin crawled at the thought of the germs and filth that ran rampant in the village. She wanted nothing more than to flee. But the call for another soul was strong, and she knew she needed to stay. Her body was already starting to weaken from her meal the night before.

While Fiona took her time setting up the vases and other pottery she'd made, Leana made her way through the market. The sooner she could find her next mate, the sooner she could leave this place.

The artists usually took their places across from the square so they could use the market as their inspiration. Leana shook her head. They would never learn true inspiration until she had hold of them.

Most of the artists that morning were older, trying to make ends meet. She skirted past them toward the younger men. The stronger they were, the longer they would feed her. They also tended to ask fewer questions as they got weaker.

There. In the back of the artists sat a young man with curly auburn hair and piercing green eyes. His strokes were sure as he painted the buildings across from him. While the others talked and laughed together, he continued to work.

Leana smoothed her dress and ran her fingers through her hair, making sure his first impression of her was perfection. She strode toward him, swaying her hips seductively. If she could get his attention from the beginning, it made everything else easier. She hated having to convince him that she was the only one he'd ever need. It took more of her essence to finally make them succumb to her.

The other artists didn't look up as she passed by. She was invisible to everyone but the man she had in her sights. It didn't stop her from brushing her fingers across the others' cheeks or whispering words into their ears. Always promising them that there was something else out there for them.

They sat up straight and looked around, dazed and wanting more. But they wouldn't get it until she was done with her current victim. This just ensured her that she would have others to come back to later.

It wasn't until she stood by his easel that the man finally glanced up at her. His eyes were even more beautiful than they'd first appeared, and Leana's breath caught. She had never seen his like.

"Excuse me, lass, but you're blocking my view." His gaze burned into her, and she stumbled out of the way.

"Sorry, I just . . . wanted to see what you were painting." She touched his shoulder, but the usual side effects of her releasing her magic on him—a sudden intake of breath, a slightly dazed expression—was absent. Who was this man?

He gestured toward the market. "I am just trying to capture humanity in all its glory. From the rich merchants to the poor villagers who simply walk through, wishing they could afford the wares."

His Irish lilt washed over her in a way that she'd never felt before. It was almost as if the intoxicating magic that she usually placed on her victims had been turned on her instead. She yearned for him to keep talking, to know everything about him.

"Is it the peasants or the merchants that you relate to the most?" Her question was sincere, but his deep, rich laughter told her that he thought she was jesting.

"Neither, actually. My family lives off in the hills away from all of this. I should be plowing the fields right now, but I escaped to do the one thing I truly enjoy." He stared at the painting. "I don't believe I'm doing the view justice, though. It's more like chicken scratches."

Leana set her hand on his shoulder as she leaned forward to look closer at the painting. She felt him stiffen, but didn't move her hand. "I believe you have captured it better than the many artists I have seen over the centuries."

His laughter filled her again. "Centuries? You cannot possibly be more than twenty. Surely you haven't traveled enough to make such a judgment."

Annoyance flowed through her. "I come here every week. I have seen my share. I have also traveled throughout much of Ireland. I can assure you, I know my art."

And then he turned his eyes toward her again. What had been a dismissal before had turned into admiration. "You have traveled? What does your family do to allow a woman of your beauty to travel? They can't be royalty or you wouldn't be on the streets at this time."

"You are not the only one who can escape your duties to follow your passions." She ran her fingers along his shoulders, smiling at the shiver that went through him. This would be quite the delightful catch. "I must get back, though. My aunt is selling pottery and I need to make sure she hasn't fallen asleep again."

The young man grabbed her hand as she stepped away from him. "Don't go. I don't even know your name."

She smiled. "It's Leana."

"I'm Conall. Return when you've checked on your aunt. I believe this is the most I've enjoyed a conversation in months." His eyes held a spark in them that made Leana weak in the knees.

"I have enjoyed it as well. I'll be back when I can." Leana walked toward the market, glancing back to make sure he was watching. Conall grinned and resumed painting. Leana shook her head and weaved her way through the stalls. She let go of the invisibility, and took a deep breath and the fatigue washed over here. Staying invisible for too long wore on her, but it was the only way she could take one victim at a time.

As she came into view of Fiona's stall, she found the old woman haggling over a large vase with a haughty nobleman.

"This took me days to have it just right. I cannot go below thirty silver." Fiona's eyes filled with tears, making Leana's temper flare up.

"That is highway robbery. I will find something at a different stall." The man began to walk away.

"Excuse me, sir." Leana's voice pierced through the noise, making the man stop and turn. He came back with desire in his eyes. Leana shuddered. It was Conall she wanted, but this man would have to do for now. "I believe you will not find another vase like this in any other stall, nor will you find it in all of Ireland. This woman weaves a bit of magic into each one that will leave you rich for the rest of your days."

Leana kept her face blank, but inside she sneered as she watched the gears turn in his head. No one would turn away the opportunity to gain even more riches, and it was clear that this man was weaker than most.

"Very well. I will pay the thirty pieces of silver, but I would like to share a meal with your daughter." He spoke to Fiona, but his eyes never left Leana.

"That is not part of the—" Fiona protested.

"It's okay, Mam." Leana patted her arm and helped wrap the vase in paper, then left the stall to walk with the man. "Let's take this to your wagon and then we can go have your meal."

The man's eyes did nothing to hide his desire as he tried to put his arm around her. A few playful swats from Leana, and he was putty in her hands.

CHAPTER TWO

LEANA

Leana made her way back to the market stall, feeling ready to burst. It was much better to take a soul over days or months rather than a few minutes, but she wanted to spend as little time with the disgusting man as she could.

Fiona sat in the back of the stall, snoring. Leana sighed and began packing up the rest of the vases. It seemed that Fiona had done well, but she was clearly worn out. The money would do her no good in life, but Leana would be able to use it for a proper burial for the woman.

Once everything was secured under the tables, Leana ducked out and hurried toward Conall. She hoped to catch him one more time before he left. Most of the others had packed their things since the sun was no longer in the right place, but Conall still painted. He looked up and waved.

"I was afraid you'd forgotten me for some merchant." His eyes danced as he stood.

Leana had underestimated his height, but it only added to his intrigue as she looked up at him. Guilt over the nobleman spiked through her, but she pushed it away. The Leanan Sidhe did not feel guilt for filling herself with the souls of others.

"Many tried, but their smiles did not compare to yours." Leana leaned in to study the painting. "This is beautiful. Wait, is that . . .?" She glanced up at him as a blush crept up her face, leaving her flustered.

"Yes, that is you. I knew it was missing something, until I saw you. I—I hope you don't mind." A look of uncertainty crossed his face.

Leana went up on her tiptoes and kissed him on the cheek, something that would have been scandalous to the town if people could actually see her. "'Tis the sweetest thing anyone has ever done for me."

Conall blushed and picked up his canvas and easel. "Pleasure to meet you. I hope we will see each other again."

"I'll be here again next week. Maybe I'll see you then." She didn't like having to wait for a week to feed on him, but the nobleman would last her for at least a few days. Waiting would also allow her to figure out why he hadn't seemed to be affected by her like other men.

"I'll see you then." He smiled one more time and

walked around the building, leaving Leana to figure out what she was feeling. Using him was supposed to be so cut and dried.

A shout rose from the market, and Leana knew it was time to go. Someone must have found the merchant's body in the back of his wagon. She pulled her cloak up over her head so no one would recognize her.

Fiona had everything loaded up in her cart by the time Leana got back to the stall. "Ah, there you are. We must leave soon or it will be too dark to travel."

"Let me take the cart this time. You're tired, and it would take you longer." Leana took her arm and helped her up inside.

"I don't know what I'd do without you." Fiona chuckled as she settled in among her vases.

Leana picked up the handles of the cart, pushed her way through the crowd, and went down a side street opposite from where the police swarmed the building. As soon as she was far enough out of the village, she turned back to make sure Fiona was asleep. Leana closed her eyes and transported them home. With a flick of her wrist, the vases were back on the shelf. She picked up Fiona and carried her to her bed, then left the cottage.

The taint of the nobleman wouldn't leave her, and she knew she had to purge his essence from her system, or she would be sick until she could feed again.

Leana pulled out the worn book that she kept with her at all times. She sat next to a pond and dangled her feet into the water. The book was the only artifact that had been passed along from the Leanan Sidhe before her, documenting who they were. The souls they'd stolen, the nations they'd managed to crumble by taking the last son from their lineage. The rules they were to obey. Not that any of them had. Feeding on the weak was just something that happened when someone asked the wrong questions.

She had the stories memorized. They'd come to her the moment she appeared on the earth. But it didn't stop her from riffling through the pages that evening. Had any others before her had feelings for the human they were bound to, or was this new?

The answer was no. Others had turned vicious and had begun craving blood along with the soul, but no one had ever fallen in love with their victim. Leana slammed her book shut. She didn't have feelings for Conall. It was just that her spell backfired. That had to be it.

Leana stood and dressed herself before walking back to the barrows. She would simply have to stay away from Conall until she no longer had feelings for him. It was imperative that she go into the partnership completely numb.

Fiona stood inside, banging pots and pans as she readied her meal. "Ah, there you are. Thank you for unpacking everything. I wasn't sure my poor body could take it."

Leana laughed with her, but felt no humor. Fiona was fading faster than Leana had expected. She set the table, slamming the plates and forks down harder than she intended.

Fiona set the dish on the table. "Eat up. I made plenty."

"Thank you." Leana detested cottage pie, but she forced it down anyway. She needed the strength after her bath tonight, and there was no one she could feed off in the area. Once her food was gone, she helped with the dishes and sent Fiona to bed with the promise that she would latch the door before going to bed herself.

A keening came from outside, chilling Leana. No. It wasn't time. She threw the door open and stalked out to where the banshee sang, welcoming Fiona home.

"No. You're too early. She has another three days." Leana's nails grew into claws, and her brilliant hair turned to flame.

The banshee stared back with mournful eyes. Her otherworldly beauty was dampened by the loss of Fiona. "'Tis how it should be. She can no longer go on. You know that."

Leana brushed away the tears that shouldn't be possible. Humans cried. Not her. "She needed those three more days."

The banshee drooped. "Leana, let her go. You can do nothing for her, and she has done nothing for you. Admit it. There was never enough of her there to keep you going."

The shock from the words felt like Leana had been slapped in the face. "I don't know what you're talking about."

"Leave her." The banshee began her keening again, dismissing Leana.

It wasn't possible. Leana had done nothing to the woman. Fiona was already weak when Leana had stumbled upon her barrow. It wasn't Leana's fault that Fiona had declined so rapidly. She was old.

Leana ran from the barrow. She didn't care where she went, but she needed to get as far away from the banshee's song as she could. She took to flight when her legs would no longer carry her. She reached the shore and finally allowed herself to rest. Sobs racked her body. Even here she could hear the melody mourning the loss of the one person who had ever truly cared for her.

Hours had passed since the sobbing had stopped. Leana stared out at the waves crashing against the sand, her hair blowing in the wind. She felt dried out. Numb. As she should be. She had been a fool to allow herself to care about a human, and she was a shame to all Leanan Sidhe before her.

But no longer. She would avoid Conall at all costs so that she wouldn't be forced to deal with emotions—good or bad. She stood and straightened her dress, then turned toward the nearest village. Surely there would be someone unable to sleep. She would be there to keep them company.

The pub was well lit with loud music and laughter floating through the open windows. Leana stepped inside and went straight to the bar. Two men sat telling stories of the ladies they'd met while out at sea, each tale a bigger lie than the last.

Leana pushed her way between them and sat on the stool. "Pardon me, loves."

They went silent, then turned to the barkeeper, arguing over who would pay for her drink. This was way too easy. Leana turned up the charm and flirted with each of them. It didn't matter which one took her home. The other would follow shortly after.

When she'd had enough flirting, she slipped off the barstool and sauntered out of the bar, watching as they scrambled to follow her. A barmaid hit one of the men with an empty bottle, screaming about how he shouldn't look at other women, which allowed the other man to leave.

He grinned and walked up to Leana, slipping his arms around her waist. "I thought I'd never get rid of him."

Leana gave her most seductive laugh as she played

with his hair, ran her fingers down his chest. "I guess he should have remembered he already had a girlfriend."

"Let's not talk." The man nuzzled her neck, then moved to her lips as he pulled her around the side of the barn, loosening his shirt as he went.

As soon as they were out of view of the bar, Leana pushed him up against the wall and kissed him, pulling on his essence. He returned her kisses hungrily and within moments, the man lay lifeless in the alleyway. Leana stepped back and smiled. Now that she had more strength, Leana pulled on the desires of the other man. Maybe, just maybe, the hole inside of her left by Fiona would be filled.

The funeral for Fiona was small, but respectable. Villagers stood around the coffin, paying their respects. Leana watched from a distance. No one had known anything about Leana, and she preferred to keep it that way. The costs for the funeral had been paid for in secret, and while they prepared Fiona, Leana took her belongings plus whatever money she could find, then left the barrows. It was time to move on.

Market day was the next day, and Leana had debated going. Conall would be there, but after the nobleman was found dead, the police force had grown. She told herself that she just wanted to continue bringing Conall under her spell, but she knew it was a lie. In the few days since Fiona's death, Leana had taken five other men, and none of them had brought the same feelings as Conall did.

Maybe it was the fact that Conall was an artist. Maybe she'd forgotten her true purpose. Maybe she should go invisible to Conall and seduce one of the other men instead. Leana shook her head. She knew it was impossible. He would always be able to see her. Even now she could feel the bond with him. It was better to just get it over with so she could move on. She could move to the other side of the country and start new. This time she would avoid dwellings that were already occupied.

Leana made sure the last tourist had left before she slipped into the dungeon of a castle. It would have to do until she could get Conall to invite her home to meet his parents. Then she would find a home nearby and focus only on him.

They had redone the inside of the castle since she'd last been inside, and she wrinkled her nose. The stones had been covered with decorative paper and tapestries, and the old fireplaces had been replaced by newer ones. Humans couldn't seem to leave the past alone. She moved from room to room, using her small amount of magic to coax the paper to fade and peel, and condensation to form on the inside of the rocks. It was easy enough to do with the rain outside. She watched in satisfaction as the floor gave way, leaving nothing but memories in the castle. This was how she remembered it from the first time she'd come to live here.

An alarm sounded from somewhere, and she sat in the corner of the room as humans rushed back and forth trying to save the castle from what they were sure was a water leak. This was much more entertaining than sleeping through the night.

She had to jump out of the way at one point when they pulled the tapestry away from the wall. She had to admit, she was a little sad that it had been destroyed. It had been embroidered by a wonderful artist.

When the excitement wore off, she moved back down into the dungeon and curled up into a ball. She'd been able to take enough essence from each of the workers, that she was content, making it easy to fall asleep.

CHAPTER THREE

CONALL

Conall watched as Leana left the market. She was beautiful beyond any woman he'd ever seen before. He'd felt the spell she'd tried to place on him, but couldn't detect her type of magic. He wasn't sure what bothered him more. That she was obviously a fairy of some kind, or that he didn't care and would do anything to have her as his own.

He hefted the easel and bag supplies and took them to his horse. His da would be expecting him at any time, and there was still an hour's travel to get home. The road was filled with vendors, and it was hard to get around them.

"Come on, Aengus, let's take to the field. We need to get out of here." Conall patted his horse's neck.

Aengus scooted around a wagon and galloped through the wheat fields, leaping over the stone walls that marked the property lines for each farm. Da would be furious if he knew that they were cutting through farmers' fields, but he'd also be angry if Conall missed dinner.

They slowed as they came upon their farmland. Night had already fallen, and he could see the lights of the house glowing in the distance as he rode into the barn. Conall took off the saddle and wiped Aengus down, then stowed his art supplies in a hidden corner in the barn, next to his crossbow and other weapons.

Mam was just putting food on the table when Conall walked in the door. He quickly washed his hands and sat down.

"I do hope you had a good reason to shirk your duties today." It was Da's way of saying he was incredibly disappointed without actually saying it.

"I went hunting. I was so close to catching a ram, but it got away at the last second." He took a few potatoes and put them on his plate. He knew Da would understand that what Conall had actually said was that he was on a hunt for a magical creature that had somehow escaped.

Da handed off the tray of roast lamb to Conall's brother Edmond. "Well, get it next time. We need storage for the winter."

Conall nodded. The farm did fairly well, but it was the bounty to catch malignant creatures that paid their bills. His dad had trained him long before Edmond and Gael were old enough to walk. He would carry on the legacy. As long as he earned the title.

"So when are you taking your brothers hunting?" Mam asked. She was always trying to get him to do things with his brothers.

"When they learn how to shoot an arrow correctly. And we all know that's not going to happen anytime soon."

Gael stabbed his fork into a potato. "Hunting isn't something I want to do anyway. Farming is a gentleman's occupation, and I plan to get myself the perfect bride and have the largest plot of land in all of Carlow County."

Conall shook his head but didn't say anything. He knew Gael could talk for hours on the subject, and there was more hunting to be done before it got too dark. Their sheep had been attacked again last night and that meant there was a water leaper somewhere around the pond.

Once dinner was over, Da distracted the boys so Conall could leave the house. He needed to get up into a tree before dark, or he'd never be able to catch the creature. He grabbed his crossbow and poison darts from the shed, then made his way up the hill to the pond. The sheep were at a distance from the pond, but he didn't put it past the water leaper to leave the water now that it had managed to snag two sheep already.

The night was quiet except for the wind blowing through the trees. Conall jumped and caught the lowest branch of the tree, then pulled himself up. He loaded the crossbow and prepared to wait.

His mind drifted back to Leana, and he wondered

again who she really was. Generally, he could tell if the magic was good or evil, but hers was hard to read. He did know that he wanted to see her again, though.

The splashing of water against the bank knocked Conall out of his meditation. He had no idea how long he'd been sitting there, but it had been worth it. The creature was here to strike again. The sound of bat wings beat against the water, propelling it to the edge of the pond. Conall made sure his ear plugs were secure—the water leaper's shrieks were deadly—and waited for the creature to come into view.

The water leaper's long thin tail snapped out of nowhere and hit one of the sheep, killing it instantly. Conall followed the tail back to the creature and shot it between its eyes, then reloaded and shot again, taking out its wing to make sure it had enough of the acid. Seconds later, the water leaper disintegrated into nothing, leaving a puff of smoke behind.

The sheep lay on its side, filled with the poison from the water leaper. Conall shot another dart into the sheep's body so that it would disintegrate as well. Otherwise it would kill whatever wild animal came by to finish it off.

Conall waited for another hour before climbing down to go back home. Da wouldn't be thrilled that they'd lost another sheep, but there wasn't much that could be done once a water leaper attacked. It was a malicious creature, and this world needed a little less evil magic floating around.

As the week progressed, Conall grew restless. Leana appeared in his dreams, and it was never enough. Maybe it was fear that she would be the next victim. He'd heard too many stories of people dying over the last little while and it made him sick to think that something could happen to her. True, the victims had been men, but it was only a matter of time before the killer would get bored.

His paintings always had her in them as the centerpiece to the picture. Her smile was easy for him to paint because he could see it so clearly. He longed to run his fingers through her hair, which was crazy because he'd only just met her. If he didn't know better, he'd think Leana had put him under a spell, but it wasn't possible. Part of being a hunter was being immune to the wiles of malicious magic.

Conall glanced up as Gael walked into the barn. He shoved his supplies into the bag and jumped up. "Does Da know you're not working?"

"Aye, and he knows you aren't either. He wanted you to rake the west pasture."

"Thanks. I'll go right now. Oh, and will you tell Mam I'll be late tonight? The pasture could take a while." Conall grabbed Aengus's saddle and got ready to head out to the field. If he hurried, he could get done in time to go see Leana. When he looked up, Gael was already gone. Trust him to take off before he heard what Conall needed him to do.

The field Da had asked him to do was large and on a hill, so the raking was hard work. Instead of riding on Aengus's back, he'd walk beside him. There was no need to tire him out by riding.

The rake broke twice, and each time Conall had to repair it before continuing on. Time was passing by quickly, and he knew that if he didn't leave soon, he'd miss Leana completely. He'd decided to skip lunch, and the hunger wore on him as he trudged up and down the hill.

By the time he finished, it was past noon. He untied Aengus and headed straight for the village. He couldn't let Leana wait for him any longer.

CHAPTER FOUR

LEANA

L eana paced the sidewalk, waiting for Conall to show up. He'd said he would be here, so where was he? The slight hope of seeing him had quickly turned to anger. How dare he keep her waiting? For that, she would take away his inspiration for the day.

Vendors called out their wares as the smells from the various food carts wafted toward her, only agitated her.

It wasn't until midafternoon that Conall finally appeared. He didn't have his easel with him this time, and instead of the clean clothes he'd worn last time, they were dirty and wrinkled. His face was unshaven, and he had circles under his eyes. He searched frantically until Leana walked toward him. His eyes lit up and he rushed over to her, pulling her into a hug.

"I almost couldn't get away from the farm. I thought I'd miss you." He squeezed her tightly to him before letting go. "Sorry. I don't know why I hugged you. That wasn't right without your consent."

Leana longed to caress his cheek, but she kept her hands clasped in front of her. "It's fine. I'm happy to see you as well."

"Da wouldn't let me leave until I got my work done. You—you were all I could think about." He ran his fingers through his hair, making it stick up straight.

The fact that he was this happy to see her should have pleased Leana, but she knew it was only because of her spell. "I thought about you as well." She shifted from one foot to the other. Usually she was too busy using her powers that she didn't have time to make conversation, and she had no idea what she was supposed to say next. "So . . . where are your art supplies?"

"At home. I didn't have time to grab them." He took her hands in his. "Come with me."

"What? Where?" Leana stepped back. Her heart beat rapidly. Strange. This had never happened before.

Conall dropped her hands. "To my home. Please. I want you to see where I live."

A thrill shot through her. "All right."

The look of surprise was quickly followed by excitement. "My horse is one block down."

He took her hand and led her to where his horse was tied up. He helped her up first, then climbed up behind her. His strong arm went around her waist, pulling her close. "Is this all right?"

Leana nodded, unable to speak. Terror seized her as

they took off down the road. She'd never been on a horse, and knew she never wanted to be again. The only thing keeping her from bolting was the arm around her.

There was little talking as they traveled because the jolting from the horse was too much. Leana was nauseated from the constant jostle, but she could feel the joy radiating off of Conall and concentrated on that.

Conall's farm was isolated from other farms, just as he had said. Leana hadn't been to this part of the countryside for decades. Not since she'd been chased by hellhounds for going after the wrong soul. The fear from the horse was replaced by a new worry. She would have to make herself visible to keep Conall from being embarrassed when he tried to introduce her to this family. It was nearly impossible that anyone would remember her from so long ago, but she didn't want to take the risk.

"Your farm is beautiful." Leana pointed toward a grove of trees in the distance. "Is there a pond up there?"

"Aye, there is. How did you know?" Conall guided her toward the farmhouse.

She winced. She'd spent several nights at that pond years ago, but he couldn't know that. "I just guessed by the trees surrounding it."

"You really have traveled everywhere, haven't you? Most people wouldn't know that." He helped her off the horse and pulled off the saddle. When he was finished, he took her hand and kissed it, then walked toward the house, oblivious to what the kiss had done to Leana's insides.

Kisses were only meant to seduce the men she wanted, but when his lips touched her skin, tingles of pleasure had shot up her arm. Feelings that she didn't know existed arose in her. Feelings that she didn't know if she wanted to dwell on or quash. This man had her so confused.

"Come on, I want you to meet my family." He led her into the house and found his mom inside the kitchen. "Mam, this is Leana."

His mother turned from the kitchen sink. She had the same eyes and smile as her son. "Welcome, Leana. It's a pleasure to meet you."

"Thank you. It's nice to meet you as well." Leana hoped that was the right thing to say. She'd watched enough humans to pick up on some polite phrases, but never had to speak with them. Conversations with her victims usually stayed short.

His mother beamed. "Conall, your father is in the shed. Can you get him to come in for dinner?"

"Aye, Mam." He kissed his mom on the cheek and then led Leana out to the barn. "Da will be a little harder to win over, but just be yourself and he'll love you."

If only he knew. Leana clung to Conall's hand as they walked into the dark shed. His father stood next to an old plow, trying to tighten one of the bolts.

"Da, Mam would like you to go in for dinner." He waited for his father to turn around, but only got a grunt. He sighed. "I would also like to introduce you to Leana."

His dad's head jerked up and he whipped around. He took a towel and wiped the grease off his hand before holding it out. "Leana, you say? Where are you from, Leana?"

Leana froze. How was she supposed to answer that? "Central Ireland. Near the Barrows."

"Ah, I've traveled there a few times meself. 'Tis beautiful there."

"It is." Leana wanted to hide behind Conall. She had faced down demons and killed people for looking at her wrong, but trying to have a normal conversation with a human had her terrified. Something was wrong with her, and she hated Conall for it.

His father dropped his tools on a table. "Let's go in and eat. Conall, were your brothers inside yet?"

"I didn't see them while I was in there." Conall squeezed Leana's hand. "I can go find them if you'd like. They were in the south field, right?"

"Aye. I'll go wash up for dinner." He nodded toward Leana before heading toward the house, whistling.

Conall shook his head. "How did you do that?"

Leana cocked her head to the side. "Do what? I did nothing."

"He has hated every woman that my brothers have brought home, but he seems to like you." He smiled down at her. "I knew you were special."

Leana returned the smile, but inside she was in turmoil. Had she used her spell on his father? Maybe. Most of the time men bent over backward to please her without her needing to do anything. But then there was Fiona . . . Leana had somehow managed to take the life of the old woman without know what she was doing.

Suddenly this was too much. She had to fight to breathe, and spots appeared in front of her eyes. "I need to walk. I'll be back."

"I can come—"

"No!" Her answer came out more forcefully than she'd wanted, and she instantly regretted it when she saw the hurt in his eyes. "I just need a moment. I have no family, and yours is so kind." The word burned in her throat. Kind was not something she was used to saying. "I'll be back, but go find your brothers and I'll meet you at your house."

Conall reached up and caressed her cheek, and a shadow passed over his eyes—part of the curse of being linked to Leana. "Go. I'll see you inside."

Leana watched him stumble toward the fields and turned away. The spell was already working. She ran until she was far enough away and then disappeared so she could fly toward the grove on the hill. Getting away from the farmhouse and the family helped her breathe better. How did humans do it? Family was so . . . stifling.

The pond was cool on her feet as she sat studying the area around her. She didn't know villages or people, but she knew the surrounding areas. She'd been here before. She didn't remember why, but something had happened.

A small fairy flitted out of the trees and landed on a rock next to her. Her big eyes watched Leana, but she stayed silent. Leana tried to ignore her, but she finally threw up her hands in aggravation.

"What do you want?" she growled.

The fairy narrowed her eyes and looked over her shoulder. Another fairy came out of the trees and another. Soon droves of fairies covered the entire grove.

Leana scrambled to her feet, her red hair turning into flame. "What do you want? I have done nothing wrong here."

A fairy came forward, his face lined with age. "Leave him. Find another victim. You have already done enough damage here."

"So I *have* been here before." Her hair went out, and her shoulders slumped. "What did I do?"

The fairy pointed toward the pond. An image formed, showing Leana with a handsome young man. They looked into each other's eyes, seeming to be in love. The boy's nose and eyes were familiar, but the hair was dark. Leana gasped. This had to be a relative of Conall's. And she remembered him now. She'd drained him slowly, dragging out the pain. When he couldn't take it anymore, she finished him in his sleep—and then destroyed the banshee who had tried to warn the family of his death.

"This family knew nothing of how their son died. You gave them no rest. We have come to avenge his death. If you do not leave Conall alone, we will make sure you never regenerate into a new Leanan Sidhe." The fairy left the grove, followed by the others. The first fairy turned to stare before disappearing.

Leana wiped the tears off her cheeks and growled. No one made her feel guilt. She formed a ball of fire in her hand and threw it as hard as she could at the trees. It did no harm to them—it was a simple illusion—but it helped release her fury.

She left the grove and stared down at the farmhouse. She could leave right now. Find someone else. She'd done it many times in the last few weeks. They hadn't brought her the same satisfaction, though. She needed someone to inspire so she could let off the extra energy she gained.

"Leana!" Conall called. "It's dark. Are you coming in?"

Leana ached to go to him. To make him happy, but she couldn't. She was too involved with him. She was a disgrace to the women who had come before her. With one last glance, she fled.

CHAPTER FIVE

CONALL

Conall's heart beat hard in his chest as he ran to find Leana. He'd watched her run this way, but there was no trace of her. Had he been wrong? Was the water leaper still alive? It could have attacked. But no, there would be other signs that it was still here. He twisted in circles, taking in the scenery. She had to be somewhere.

After checking the pond for the fourth time, he raced back to the house to see if she'd come back while he was gone.

"Any sign of her?" Da asked.

"No. She couldn't have walked home. She lives . . ." Where did she say she lived? All he knew was that she traveled often. "She headed toward the pond."

Da grabbed his hat and shoes. "Then we'd better go look for her up there."

Conall sprinted ahead, but inside he knew she was gone. They searched through the trees and took a branch to dredge the pond, but she was nowhere to be found.

He sat on one of the large boulders and rested his elbows on his knees, defeated.

Da set his hand on Conall's shoulder. "We'll find her."

Despair filled Conall, and he couldn't say anything as Da walked away. It wasn't that he thought she was dead. He knew he'd have felt it the moment it happened through the bond he seemed to have with her. It was that she'd left without a goodbye and taken his heart with her.

Conall sat near the water's edge waiting for just the right moment. The waves lapped up against the beach just a few feet away. He sat still, watching a kelpie try to lure a young girl onto its back. He needed the girl to move to get a good shot, but if he made a sound, the kelpie would spook and take off. This was the second girl this week that had been caught in its snare, and Conall wasn't about to let the kelpie get her.

The girl glanced back toward her parents who were at a dinner party, then ran for the kelpie with outstretched arms. Conall took the shot, sending a harness directly at its face. The harness had a cross carved into it, which trapped the kelpie. He then followed it with a dart. The kelpie let out a shriek of pain before moving back into the water. Conall ran forward and grabbed the girl before she could follow it and drown.

She sobbed into Conall's shoulder as he took her back to her parents who had just realized that she was gone. Conall passed her off, then left the party before any questions could be asked. They would find a letter tucked into her dad's pocket later that night describing what had happened. Conall had hoped he'd have the chance to deliver it.

It had been weeks since he'd seen or heard from Leana. He'd thrown himself into hunting to get over her, which was good for the sake of the people. Deaths had picked up throughout the country. They seemed random, except that each of the victims seemed to have dropped at the prime of life with no sign of trauma. He'd worried about a vampire, but there were no fang marks.

After one more patrol around the area, he returned home. Mam had dinner waiting for him, but his brothers were nowhere to be found.

"How was your hunt, dear?"

"I managed to snag a few rabbits today. I figured you could make a stew for dinner tomorrow night." He gestured toward his bag that sat by the door.

His mom sighed in exasperation. "I told you not to just leave your hunt in your bag."

"Sorry." He shoveled the meat pie into his mouth, barely pausing to chew before he swallowed. He hadn't eaten since breakfast that morning. "Where is everyone?"

"Out with friends. Da is in the workshop. He could use some help once you're done." She frowned as she skinned the rabbits. "I'm worried about him. He's working too hard while you're gone."

Conall stood to take his dishes to the sink. He bent and kissed her cheek. "I'll go out right now. Planting is nearly done and then he'll be able to relax."

"Unless he goes hunting with you."

"That's a possibility." Conall put on his coat and hat before trudging out to the workshop where his dad worked on an old plow. "Hey, Da. I got him."

"Well done. Catching your first kelpie is not an easy feat." He tossed Conall a wrench. "Tighten that side."

Conall bent down and tightened the bolt. "I think I'm going to go into the village tomorrow. They're saying more have died or gone missing there."

"I was going to suggest the same thing." Da paused. "And the girl?"

Conall shrugged. "She obviously doesn't want to be with me. If she's there . . . I don't know what I'll say."

"She's beautiful."

"I know. But she left without saying goodbye, and she hasn't made contact since. I'd say that's a pretty good indication that she wants nothing to do with me."

Da chuckled. "I'd say you're right."

"Mam's worried about you."

"I know. She always has been." He put the tools down. "All right. That's the best we're going to do for tonight. Let's go in."

Conall waited for Da to grab his coat, then turned off the light as he left. He ached to have the same familiar relationship as his parents had. But if that meant letting go of the one person he cared about to get it, would he do it?

CHAPTER SIX

LEANA

Leana stared at the young musician as he slouched over his music. She had found him while wandering through the forests near Kilkenny, and had followed him back to the village. Within a few days, she knew every moment of his day. So far she had sent him inspiration from a distance. His music had improved immensely, and the nobles had taken notice.

It was nearly time for him to have his evening walk, and that's when she would finally introduce herself to him. While Conall was tall, broad shouldered, and handsome, this young man was short and thin. He was still muscled from carrying his instrument everywhere he went, so he would do well. Not as well as Conall—no. She shook her head to get his face out of her mind. Conall was a failure on her part, and she didn't need to be reminded of that.

The young man packed up his things and stood to stretch. Leana smirked. He was right on time. As he passed by, she stumbled out of the alleyway and fell at his feet. The boy was constantly distracted, and Leana knew this was the only way to get his attention.

He leaned down and set his things on the ground before rolling her over. "Miss? Are you okay?"

His voice was soft as he brushed the hair from her face. His intake of breath nearly made her smile, but she simply fluttered her eyelashes. He was as good as hers.

"You saved me." She took his hand as he helped her up, then cried out in pain. "My ankle, I think I did something to it."

The young man scooped her up in his arms. "Where is your home?"

"I was just passing through, hoping to find a place to stay." She leaned her head against his chest. His heart rate sped up, making Leana smirk. She had him in the palm of her hands.

"I'll take you to my home. My mam can help you."

"But what about your things?" Leana pointed down at his instrument. "What will you do with that?"

The young man paused. "I will have to come back and get them."

He walked toward the edge of town. "What is your name?"

"Leana."

"That is a beautiful name. I'm Ennis." He knocked on the door to an old white house. "Why are you traveling alone?"

Leana paused for a moment. People asked too many questions. "I needed to get away from someone, and I left with nothing."

Ennis pushed the door open. "Mam must not be home from the market. I'm going to set you on the couch and then go back to get my violin."

"You're leaving me here alone?" Leana pouted.

"I'll be right back." He made sure she was settled on the couch before leaving the house.

Leana glanced around the room, taking in the decor. The furnishings were simple, and there was music scattered all over the tables and chairs. She picked up one of the pages and hummed the tune. It was beautiful, but there was something off in the middle.

"Ah, that old piece. I've given up on it." Ennis set his violin down on the couch, then sat next to Leana, his shoulder brushing hers. "There is something here I can't quite . . ." His eyes lit up. "I think I have it."

Ennis spent the next hour rewriting the song, and when he was finished, Leana knew that it would be a huge success. She breathed in deeply, feeding on his excitement. Now this was perfect. She'd missed how alive she felt.

"This is beautiful music. What else do you have?" She ran her hand along his arm and watched as he closed his eyes in pleasure.

He jumped and leaned forward. "There are a few

others that I've been working on for months. My mam continues to buy me paper, thinking that I will be a brilliant composer, but I have yet to write anything that I would consider good. Until the piece I just finished."

"Well, let's go over some others." Now that she'd had a taste of his soul, she ached for more. She hadn't felt this energized since the artist at the lake.

"They're no good. Look here. I know I need something extra, but I . . ." He trailed off and grabbed his pen to add the missing pieces to it. Once he'd finished with that, he moved on to the next piece, then the one after that.

Leana watched in satisfaction as she slowly pulled his soul from him. Energy flowed through her and she felt better than she had for weeks. "Will you play your violin for me?"

"Of course." Ennis pulled the violin out of its case and tuned it. The melody was light and happy and his voice blended in wonderfully as he sang. When he finished, Leana clapped in delight.

"That was beautiful. Good enough to play in front of the queen." But Leana knew that wouldn't happen. She could already see a marked difference in him. He would be lucky if he got to say goodbye to his mother. She stood. "I should probably get going. Your mother isn't here, and it's getting late. Thank you for your help."

Ennis jumped up. "You can't leave with a hurt ankle. Stay here. Mam won't mind."

"It just needed to rest. I'll be fine. Thank you." She kissed him on the cheek, lingering just a little longer than she should have.

A light groan escaped from Ennis as he turned to press his lips against hers. Leana leaned into him, wrapping her arms around his neck. He wound his fingers through her hair and wrapped his other arm around her waist.

Leana felt him weaken as they stood locked in the embrace. She pulled him down onto the couch so that he wouldn't collapse. She'd hoped to make this last longer, but he was too easy. She would have to find someone else to feed her hunger.

Ennis pulled away. "I just thought of a song. I need . . . to write . . ."

Leana let go of him and released the spell so he could finish his one last masterpiece. Once he was gone, she would make sure it got into the right hands. He would be famous, but never know the joy his music would bring to people.

As he finished the last few notes, he dropped the quill, clearly exhausted. His skin hung loosely on his already thin frame, and his eyes were sunken in.

Leana took the quill and put it in his hand. "Don't forget to sign your page."

He slowly moved it to sign his name, the last letter running off the paper. He reached out and cupped

Leana's face in his hand. "I don't know what you are, but thank you for letting me finish my work before I go."

Leana nodded, unable to speak. She kissed him one more time, releasing his soul into hers, then gathered up his music. The front door rattled, announcing his mother's arrival, so she slipped out the back door. A tear escaped as she heard his mother's scream turn into sobs.

The air was cool as Leana hurried down the street. She set the pile of music on the step of the castle, then hid. It was a few minutes before the royal guard opened the door and looked around before finding the pages on the mat. He riffled through them, as he closed the door behind him.

There was nothing left for her here. It was time to go. She had taken the lives of too many people recently, and she needed to hide out for a while.

CHAPTER SEVEN

CONALL

Conall had just drifted off to sleep when he heard a knock at the door downstairs. He closed his eyes again, hoping to fall back asleep, but the knock became more insistent. Mam was a heavy sleeper, and Da had gone out of town on business, so it was up to Conall to see what was going on.

He pulled on a pair of pants and went to find out who it was. A man stood outside, nervously twisting his hat in his hands. When Conall didn't answer the door, the man knocked again. Conall pulled the door open, startling him.

"Do you often call on people after midnight?" Conall tried to control the annoyance in his voice, but it was hard when he'd worked a full day on the farm, followed by a few hours tracking another kelpie sighting. Apparently the harness hadn't done its trick, and Conall wasn't about to let it get away again.

"No, but I arrived just now from Scotland. I have been unable to contact your father, and we are in need of a hunter as soon as possible. We have a Cu Sith who won't leave the cattle alone, and we worry that it will go after our families next."

Conall stared at the man. "And you have no one there who can take care of it?"

"Many have tried, but they have failed every time. If your father is unavailable, do you know of someone who might be willing to help?" The man twisted his hat in his hands, and he appeared as though he would drop it at any time.

He could turn the man away right now, but Conall was intrigued. He moved so the man could enter and gestured toward the couches. He held up a finger to tell him to wait and then listened near the stairs to make sure his mother was still asleep.

"I have taken over my father's position in many ways, and I could help, but again, why have you come here instead of finding a hunter in your country?" Conall rested his elbows on his knees.

The man rubbed his face before answering. "This Cu Sith is not the only malignant creature walking the land right now. Two of our hunters were killed in this latest hunt, and we have yet to find someone else willing to take over. Word has spread that there were a couple of fine hunters here."

"We're currently looking for a few creatures here. Leaving would mean they can find more victims." Conall hated turning him down, but until the kelpie and whoever was killing in this country were captured, he couldn't leave. "I'm sorry you've traveled all this way."

The man nodded and stood, handing Conall a card. "If you reconsider, I'm leaving tomorrow."

"Thank you." Conall opened the door and watched the man trudge toward his horse. He looked like a man with a large burden on his shoulders. Part of Conall wanted to run after him and head off on a new adventure, but the other part knew he was needed here.

Still, a new country meant new adventures. He had ached to paint the lands he'd only heard of in books, and this would allow him to do it. Maybe if he were able to rid Ireland of these creatures, he would follow the man in the spring when the sea was safe to travel again.

CHAPTER EIGHT

LEANA

Winter came, making it next to impossible to find someone to feed off of. Leana took to wandering the halls of the local university. She remained invisible as she gathered bits and pieces from the people who sat at the tables to study. It wasn't what she wanted, but she needed something to keep her mind off Conall.

She had gone back to his farm a few times over the last few months, hoping to catch a glimpse as his family worked out in the fields, gathering in the harvest. He was there at times, and she could get him to look around to where she stood, but he always looked back down. It was a mystery to her how he was able to resist her, and the hurt that came from it was unlike anything she'd felt before.

At least with the university, she was able to find a place to stay—an old dorm that they were renovating—and she had access to all the souls she could ever want. All except for the one she truly ached to have.

Rumors began to float on the winds that there was a hunter in the land. A hunter who went for the dark creatures like her. She'd been able to avoid the hunters of the past, and had enjoyed seducing a few just to get them off the trail of her dear kelpie friends, but this one was different. It was said that the darkest of the creatures had either gone back to the fairy world or they'd been destroyed.

It was late one night when Leana slipped into the university library. She needed to find a creature to help divert the hunter's attention away from her. Someone who would do the same damage she could do, someone who wouldn't leave a trace. This institute was lacking in the mythology department, but she hoped it would still guide her.

Leprechauns, clurichauns, pooka, all well known, none of which would help her. The selkies were difficult to find, while the hunter had already found a way to defeat kelpies. Leana slammed the book shut and moved on to the next one.

The next book was filled with beings that seemed to be more of what she wanted. Vampire-like creatures were her best bet, but they were extremely hard to track down. She wrote down what she could find and then moved on.

As the sun began to appear on the horizon, Leana closed the last book and set it on the shelf. She'd found a few options, and it was time to leave before the library began to fill with students. They were always too tired in the morning and left her sluggish after trying their essence.

She wrapped her cloak around her and lifted the hood over her hair to hide her appearance before leaving the room. The door creaked shut, making her cringe. When she turned, a man stood there, looking at her in surprise.

"May I help you?" he asked.

"I—was just looking for something in the library, but I can come back later." She searched his face, admiring the graying hair and small lines that had begun to form around his eyes. "Do you work here?"

He nodded. "I am the librarian. What are you looking for? Perhaps I can help."

"I searched the entire library for mythology and it was lacking in what I needed. Please excuse me." She pushed past him toward the old dorm.

"I can help with that. I have a master's in mythology."

Leana forced herself not to smile. He knew all about mythology, and yet he couldn't see who she actually was. "Have you written much on the myths in this country? Or is it all just studies?"

"Much of my work has been on collecting any books I can find, but at some point, yes, I'd like to write it." He adjusted his glasses.

"Well, then, I believe we can be of great service to each other." Leana smiled as she followed him into the library. He would do quite nicely.

CHAPTER NINE

CONALL

Conall forced the dullahan off him and grabbed his sword off the ground. "You won't be getting my soul any time soon."

The headless man laughed as he lunged again. "You will not win, you fool."

"I thought you were supposed to be silent." Conall shrugged. "I guess that just makes this more fun." He pulled a stake made of pure gold and aimed at the dullahan's heart. His throw was perfect and hit the dullahan where his heart should have been.

The dullahan stared down at the stake and laughed as he pulled it out, completely unharmed. "Well done, hunter. You have done your research."

Conall stood in shock. If this wasn't the dullahan, then what was it? Wait—he peered closely at the creature. Yes, there was a definite aura around it. The pooka. He ducked behind a boulder and unstrapped his crossbow from his back. He rolled his eyes as the pooka laughed and mocked him for his folly. He put a bolt into the crossbow and shot it directly at the creature. The bolt hit the pooka and released a net, capturing it. The thing let out a loud roar and fought violently.

"You were saying?" Conall walked forward and nudged the net with his foot. "Like my newest weapon? No? Well, it's going to help me get what I need." He crouched down. "I believe I have two requests I can get from you. First, I want you to leave this island and never return again. And second, I want you to take your dark friends with you. Understand?"

The pooka transformed back into its normal horselike state. "You cannot demand that of us."

"I believe I can. Now, I'm going to release this, and you'd better go. Because if you stick around, I won't be so kind." He yanked on the net, pulling it into itself and watched as the pooka galloped away. Conall just hoped he'd take his friends with him, but he doubted that would happen.

The shame of mistaking the creature's true identity washed over him, but he couldn't be too hard on himself. Shape-shifters were hard to identify, and the pooka was one of the best.

Conall jogged toward his farm, making sure there was plenty of space between him and where the pooka had been before he whistled. Aengus was a good horse, but he still spooked easily. It was another minute or two before Conall heard the familiar whinny, and another minute before he finally galloped up.

"There you are. Let's get home." Conall climbed up and hooked his crossbow over his shoulder, then checked the knives in his belt. It was becoming more widely known that he was the hunter, and he had to keep an eye out for any creatures who wanted to take him on. Imps were especially fun to deal with as their inky black skin helped them blend into the darkness of the night.

Lights were on at the house when Conall came over the hill. He grinned as he urged Aengus into a gallop for the last mile. Da was back from his hunt. Conall quickly rubbed down his horse with a promise that he would take care of him more tomorrow, then ran into the house.

"Da. You're back." He wrapped him in a hug, then dropped into a kitchen chair. "How did it go? Were you able to find anything?"

Da shook his head. "Whatever this is has done well keeping their tracks hidden as you said. No trace of magic, no sign of struggle. I do have one idea, though."

Conall perked up. "What is it?"

"Leanan Sidhe. 'Tis one of a few that could have done this, but she seems to fit the best. The only problem is, the only people who see her are the victims themselves, so we have no documentation of what she looks like. Which makes her the perfect suspect." Da pushed a paper over to Conall. "This was found at a library not long ago."

Notes had been taken in scrawled handwriting, done by someone who had obviously not done much writing before. "This explains a few things, but why would she write notes about herself?"

"I wondered the same thing, which is why I've put her on the bottom of the list. But get this. The librarian who was found had a large pile of parchment next to him, and he'd written a book on various creatures. The library reports that he went missing two weeks ago, which means he was most likely holed up writing the book until his death."

"So maybe it wasn't the creature who wrote this note?" Conall held up the paper. "Maybe it was the librarian?"

Da shook his head. "The handwriting doesn't match. Listen, I've heard of similar cases of a creature like this in parts of Scotland. Are you still in contact with the man who came to visit?"

"I have his card upstairs, why?" Conall continued to stare at the note in front of him. Who was the creature that did this?

"I want you to go. We need to learn more, and quite frankly, I want you to move on with your life. You need to see the world before you rot away on this farm, and this is the perfect opportunity."

Conall's head jerked up. "But what will you do? You can't handle all these creatures by yourself."

Da chuckled. "I've done it since I was younger than you. I can handle it. Besides, you've taken care of most of the threats already."

The thought of going was definitely tempting. And now that he had another reason to go, it was hard to say no. The dull ache in his heart reminded him that it would mean leaving Leana, but she had managed to stay away from him for this long, and it was easier to keep it this way.

"All right. I'll go. But if I return home to find that Gael or Edmond has taken over my place, I'll be very unhappy." Now that the decision was made, Conall could feel the excitement wash over him. He didn't want to wait to hear from the man, he wanted to leave right away.

"Don't worry about that. They have their own paths to follow." Da clapped him on the back. "I have all the necessary papers ready so that you can leave as soon as your things are gathered. The hard part is letting your mam know that you're leaving."

Conall laughed. "I figure since you took care of the paperwork, you could take care of that part too."

"Nice try." Da stood and went to the cupboard to get a glass. "I'll give you two days to get everything done and say your goodbyes. That should give the courier enough time to get the letter to your friend."

"Thanks, Da. I'll head into town tomorrow to grab what I need." Conall headed up to his room, making a list of things he'd need to do before he left. Leana drifted through his mind, but he knew he needed to leave without seeing her, or he would change his mind and choose to stay with her instead.

CHAPTER TEN

LEANA

Leana stood near the back of the crowd waiting as the symphony began to play. The music she had helped Ennis compose was being performed, and as she listened, she watched to see how the others reacted. Some wiped eyes, while others just stood and listened. It had a beautiful melody, with a harmony that complemented it perfectly. It was her favorite of the many compositions she'd inspired over the centuries, and she wanted everyone else to feel the same way.

When it finally ended, the crowd was silent for a moment before clapping wildly.

Satisfied with the reception of the composition, Leana turned to leave. Conall stood behind her, tall and handsome. She shrank inside herself, not knowing how he would react to seeing her. It had been too long, and the ache she'd felt since then had lightened dramatically.

He smiled, but it was tinged with sadness. "Hello, Leana."

"Hello. What are you doing in town? And so far

away from your home?" Leana rubbed her arms in the cold. She wasn't supposed to feel the wintery chill, but she'd let down her guard.

Conall stared off into the distance. "I needed to buy supplies from our small village, but I was drawn here instead. I thought it was to say goodbye to the marketplace that I love so much, but when I saw you . . . I knew it was you who I needed to see."

Leana swallowed hard. She'd never walked away from a man once she had them under her spell, so this was completely new. "I'm sorry."

"You're not. I see it in your eyes. I don't know what I did that night. Maybe I pushed too hard to have you meet my family, but I thought things were going well. When you didn't come back . . . we searched the woods for days to find your body." He choked on the last word. "The worst part is that I knew deep down that you were gone by choice."

"I *am* sorry that I hurt you. But I am not sorry I left. I don't know how to feel. I don't know how to express myself. And most of all, I don't know how to let someone care for me." Leana's voice was flat as she said it, but she knew it was true.

Conall leaned down suddenly and kissed her. His lips were insistent, and brought a passion that Leana had never experienced before. She was used to kisses from men who were pulled in by her spell. They brought what she needed, but this. This was different. She'd lived for centuries, but no kiss had ever brought an excitement like this one. What she did know was that when he pulled away, she felt a piece of her go with him.

He ran his thumb across her cheek. His eyes were tired, and he'd thinned out, meaning that her spell had worked on him. And for the first time ever, she realized she didn't want his soul in this way. Not his.

"Leana, I know nothing of where you come from, or who you are, but I know you are dangerous to be around. There's nothing I want more than to have you by my side, but I can't. I'm glad I got to see you one more time, but I'm leaving."

"Where—?"

"I can't tell you. I don't want you to follow." He leaned down and kissed her one more time, this one more delicious than the first. And then he was gone.

Leana ran down the alley to find him, but there was no trace. She closed her eyes, hoping to sense him, but there was nothing. She let out a sob and sunk to the ground. She'd failed in every way possible. *Don't get involved, lose all emotion, and most of all, never under any circumstances fall in love.*

Those words echoed through her mind over and over again. They were written many times throughout the book she kept in her robe, and for centuries she'd lived by them. Curse him. Curse humans all together.

Leana took breaths to calm herself down, but peace wouldn't come. She stood and wiped her eyes just as a man came around the corner. His eyes were filled with concern as he took in her appearance.

"I thought I heard crying. Are you hurt?"

"I—I'm fine. I just feel so lost." Another tear ran down her cheek, and she cursed at it as well. Tears were weakness, as was sadness. Conall had ruined who she was by making her care.

He helped her stand, then put his arm around her and guided her out of the alley. "I'll take you to the church to get warm and we can talk. No one can hurt you there."

Leana froze. She couldn't go into the church. "I— can we talk somewhere else? I feel my problems aren't something that can be helped there."

The man searched her face before finally nodding. "Very well. Let's see if I can help you out."

The tears were replaced by a hesitant smile, forcing herself to remember who she was, and what she needed to survive. He could help. He just didn't understand that it would be the last thing he'd ever do.

CHAPTER ELEVEN

CONALL

The emptiness that filled Conall overshadowed the excitement he'd felt for the trip. But he knew he was making the right decision in leaving. The thought of settling for someone else was too much, so he would hunt.

As soon as he said goodbye, he ducked around the corner and waited for her to run past before going the other way to climb on Aengus. The taste of her lips still lingered, making him feel more alive than he ever had before.

The ship would be taking off in a few hours, and he still needed to get Aengus back to the farm. Da needed him too much to sell off before he left. Since it wasn't a market day, the road was fairly clear back to his house. It was bittersweet, knowing it would be months or years before he would return to the place where he was born. The place where his family had lived for generations.

He climbed off Aengus as soon as he arrived at the barn, then took his time brushing him down.

"Be good for Da. I'll be back as soon as I can." He patted Aengus on the back and walked in to say goodbye to his mam.

Mam wiped her tears and smiled as he walked into the house. She'd taken the news much easier than either he or Da had expected. "Take care, son. Return soon."

Conall kissed her and hugged her tightly. "I'll write often and be back as soon as the contract is done."

Gael and Edmond hugged him next before he and Da went out to the horse and wagon. Mam waved as they left, and Conall waved until he could no longer see her. The trip to Dublin went quicker than normal because of Da's steeds that he'd paid top dollar for.

Da climbed down from the wagon and made sure Conall had everything he needed. "Good luck over there. They have creatures native to their own country, so some of your usual fighting techniques may not work."

"I'll keep an eye out for them. I have the book you gave me to document what I find." He shook his da's hand, then walked up the plank into the ship. Crew members pushed past the passengers to do their jobs, and Conall couldn't help grinning as he moved on to his next adventure. Maybe he'd finally heal from the heartache once and for all.

The coast of Scotland came into view just as the sun rose. Conall sat on deck sketching the horizon, wanting to remember every moment as he arrived in a new country. The trip had been uneventful, despite the attempts from a few sea monsters that tried to attack the ship. His nets had been enough to distract them, and the wind was perfect to make good time.

The ship's deck slowly came to life as passengers woke and made their way to the dining hall to eat before it was time to disembark. Conall packed up his things and headed down to his cabin to gather the rest of his luggage. The sea made his stomach queasy, and breakfast was the last thing on his mind.

A large tentacle rose out of the water a few hundred yards away, but the creature knew better than to attack the ship. Conall's darts had taught it the lesson quickly enough. He just hoped it would keep the beisht krone far away from the ship. The sailors had kept him up one night, telling him about the beast with the black head and how many friends they'd lost to it.

Conall shook his head and looked away, watching as the coast came closer. They were near enough that he could see activity as things were prepared there for the landing. He rubbed his chest, trying to rid himself of the ache that had continued to grow as he moved away from Ireland.

He was the first passenger off the ship, ready for adventure. Da hadn't heard back from the man, but Conall had the address on the card that the man had given him. He looked around for the nearest policeman and made his way over to him.

"Excuse me? I'm looking for this address." He pointed it out on the card.

"You have a ways to go. Head straight and get yourself a horse, then you're going to want to continue inland to the next village. They'll be able to tell you from there where to find this man."

"Thank you." Conall picked up his things and walked toward the stables, growing tired faster than he should have going up the hill. His chest hurt as he gasped for air and had to stop to catch his breath. He hoped he wasn't catching a cold.

The stables were nearly bare by the time he entered the office to ask for a horse. Three other people he recognized from the ship were in line. An old, stooped man handed the stable boy a paper and sent the people back with him, then turned to Conall.

"What can I do for you?" He held his shaking hand over the notebook in front of him.

"I need to buy a horse. Are there any for sale?" There was no need to borrow a horse when he planned to travel for most of the time he was in the country.

The man's eyebrows shot up. "We have beautiful horses you can borrow—"

"I appreciate that, but I really do want to buy it. I have the money to cover it."

"That'll be a hundred pounds." The man held out his hand, a greedy glint to his eye.

Conall knew it was way too high for any of the horses they had to have cooped up in the stable, but he pulled out the coins anyway. He'd saved up for years for his dowry, but he now knew that marriage would probably never happen.

The man counted the coins out before scrawling something on a paper. He handed it to the stable boy who had just come back. "Get him Conan and make sure he's saddled correctly."

The boy's eyes widened as he glanced between them, but said nothing as he walked back into the stables. It was clean enough, and the horses seemed well-cared for as

Conall passed by the few that were left. The boy saddled the horse and handed Conall the reins.

"Thank you." Conall gave him a couple of pounds before heading out of the stables. The bite to the air was unusual for this time of year, but at least he wouldn't get too warm on his travels.

The paths were well-worn as he made his way to the next village. He hoped the trip hadn't been in vain and that the man still required his help. Conall rubbed his chest to try to ease that ache, and then headed toward his new adventure.

CHAPTER TWELVE

LEANA

Leana glanced around before running to the small cave in the hills. She knocked on the door and waited for an answer. It was possible that the accounts were correct, but Leana wanted to find out for herself.

As she waited, Leana became less certain of her quest. She turned to leave, but stopped suddenly. The door to the cave had creaked open. She hurried back.

"Hello? Carman?" she called out.

"What is it you want?" The voice was raspy and cold, and it sent shivers through Leana.

Leana cleared her throat. "I must speak with you. I am the Leanan Sidhe, and I've come to ask for your help."

A woman who seemed as old as the earth itself stood in the doorway. Leana felt like a small child next to her, and indeed she was, compared to Carman.

"Ah, my child. Come in." She moved out of the way, allowing Leana to duck into the cave.

The cave was dim and smelled of old food and herbs, along with the earthiness Leana was used to after dwelling in barrows for so long. Carman limped across the living space and pulled down two mugs.

Leana stood in the center of the room, not knowing what to do with herself. "Where are your sons?"

"Fools got themselves destroyed a century or so ago." Her cackle turned into a cough. "Tea?"

"Yes, thank you." Leana stepped closer to the counter where Carman stood. "So the legends were true, then."

"All legends are true to a point. They only said they caught me with the boys so they could sleep better at night." She dumped a spoonful of herbs into the mug and poured water over them. The air filled with a pungent, rather unpleasant aroma.

Leana hesitated before taking the mug. She'd fed on the souls of men—this couldn't be much worse. Carman waited for her to take a drink, so Leana brought it to her lips and took a sip. The flavor was a stark contrast to the smell. It was almost too sweet for her taste, but calmed her emotions. Emotions that should not have existed.

"Now, I assume you're here because of a man. What is it you want? Fire? Drowning?"

Leana's eyebrows shot up. "What? No. Nothing like that. I can . . . you do know who I am, right?"

"I do. I also know a spurned woman when I see one, and honey, you have all the signs. But if you *are* the

Leanan Sidhe, then why are you here? Do away with him. Humans are vile creatures."

"I . . ." Leana paused. "I want to forget him. I can't do what I do if I'm feeling things." She rubbed her forehead. "I don't like feeling things. Make me numb. Make me . . . make me who I was before I met that man."

"No."

Leana blinked. "What?"

"I can't change that. And if I could, I wouldn't. You want to go back to doing your duty, to inspire artists, right? Being numb and forgetting everything you've learned is not the way to do it. Think of the music or art that could be inspired by fear or anger or heartbreak. You've focused on the passion, but there are other ways." Carman wiped down the counter. "I miss my boys. Terribly. I used that anger and sorrow to get back at the families who destroyed them. Every day I live with that sorrow. And now I know that the families I destroyed feel that same way. And I wouldn't change it."

Shock and disgust filled Leana. "These are human emotions. Why would you use them like that?"

"Because the best way to break a human is to go at their emotions. And what better way to do that than to know how it feels yourself?"

Leana stepped back. "I thought . . . I don't know what I thought. But I can't just embrace these feelings. They hurt too much."

"I know. Use them." The amused expression on

Carman's face only angered Leana more. "Look, I can see I'm not going to convince you. But I refuse to take away something you've learned in your own way. Go find the dullahan or someone else, but they will help you no more than I have."

Leana curtsied to show the respect Carman deserved and then stormed out of the cave. She growled at the laughter she heard behind her. How dare the woman laugh at Leana's pain? It had taken weeks to find the exact location of Carman's cave—she'd had to do countless acts that made her shudder, and all she got out of it was that she should use the very thing she wanted to be rid of.

CHAPTER THIRTEEN

CONALL

C onall stared down at the lake, waiting for some sign that the Cu Sith had come to hunt. He'd spent a few weeks attempting to track it, but it was nearly impossible. The only time it made itself known was when it was about to attack.

The telltale yowl appeared to the south of Conall, making him whip around. How had the beast gotten past him? He swore and ran toward his horse, pulling his crossbow off his back. His breaths came in gasps, but he wasn't going to stop until he got this beast.

A small cabin sat nestled in the mountains, and it appeared that the beast had chosen it as its next attack— exactly what Conall feared. If the creature were to get in, he would take the mother and her new baby back to the fairy world. And Conall wasn't about to let that happen.

The howling meant he only had a few minutes to stop the beast. Conall urged his horse forward, wishing he had Aengus. This horse spooked too easily, and he didn't have time or energy to run the rest of the way on his own.

Pounding came from ahead as the beast tried to get inside the house. The wail of a baby broke through the howl, which made the Cu Sith angrier. Conall forced the horse into a gallop and jumped off the moment the horse panicked and reared back on its hind legs.

Just another hundred yards and he'd be within range. Conall sprinted the best he could as the pressure on his heart and lungs squeezed harder. He ducked behind a tree, making sure the bolts were secure. As the beast leapt at the front door again, Conall shot the iron bolt directly at its shaggy white head.

The angry howl turned to pain as it whipped around, its glowing red eyes searching the dark for whatever shot it. Conall aimed and shot another bolt into the center of its forehead, instantly killing it. He shot two more bolts just to be sure. Moments later, the body turned to dust and floated away, leaving vines and thorns in its wake. Conall made a face. He'd heard that fairies would leave beautiful flowers or clover behind, so it only made sense that this dark creature would bring noxious weeds to the world.

Conall stood, but instantly collapsed. His heart thudded in his ears as he fought to breathe. He pulled himself forward, trying to get to the cabin to make sure the mother and child were okay. As darkness overtook him, his one regret was that he would never get to tell Leana just how much he loved her.

CHAPTER FOURTEEN
LEANA

It was in the early hours of the morning when Leana felt the bond to Conall become stronger. She jerked to her feet and turned toward the Northeast. Conall was back. Emotions warred within her. He had said he wanted to stay away from her, but would he reject her if they were to meet again? Maybe. But it was also possible he would be happy to see her after his adventures.

She'd traveled over acres of land before she realized what she was doing and stopped. It was foolish to go after a human who had rejected her. In reality, he should be dead for breaking the pact between the two of them. One man had attempted to ensnare her with a contract where he could reject her and make her his slave. Unfortunately for him, she was too quick and he was gone before he could get the words out of his mouth.

Leana stood in an empty field, unable to decide what she should do. She wanted to see him more than she should ever want to see a human. The ache in her heart told her that she needed him near.

But she'd already pushed her limits. She'd fed on too many artists in a short amount of time, and while the country was abuzz with the masterpieces that had suddenly erupted in music, art, and literature, it was tinged with sadness over the deaths of these young prodigies. It was only a matter of time before people would begin to go from the idea of a serial killer to the supernatural.

It was time to go into hiding. She'd hibernated for years before, and after the feast she'd had, she could do it again for a few decades. Going after Conall wasn't in the equation. She turned away from Conall's presence and headed for the barrows where Fiona once lived, determined that this was what she wanted to do.

And then Leana noticed something else. The life force she'd taken from Conall had gone from a dull ache to sheer agony. Conall was in pain and if something didn't happen soon, he would be gone forever. And after losing Fiona, she wasn't about to let that happen.

Miles disappeared below her as she flew toward the old farmhouse where Conall lived. She avoided the grove of trees where the fairies were surely waiting for her and went straight to the door. She kept invisible as she watched through the window. His mother kept her face hidden as sobs racked her body. His father held her tightly. Conall lay on the couch, pale and half the man he'd been the last time Leana had seen him. And it was because of Leana.

While she wanted to burst in and save him right then, she knew it would be a bad idea. It was torture waiting for the dark of night after everyone was asleep. His mom slept in the chair next to his side, his hand clasped in hers. Leana opened the door slowly, careful not to allow it to creak. They wouldn't see her, but she also didn't want to alarm them.

Her steps were silent as she went to his side. She knew before she felt his pulse that he was nearly gone. Being away from Leana had nearly killed him. What she was about to do could finish him off, or it could give him another chance to love her. One more glance at his mother told Leana that she was doing the right thing, even if there were dire consequences involved.

She bent down and kissed his lips. But this time, instead of pulling his soul, she pushed hers into him. She had plenty to share at the moment, and losing him meant that life was no longer worth living.

Leana pulled away, staring at his perfect features as she waited to see if she'd been too late. Conall gasped for air and began convulsing as the blood began rushing through his body again. Leana caressed his cheek, trying to help his body calm down.

"Conall?"

Leana jumped back as his mom dropped to her knees and scooted toward him. She brushed his hair away from his face and patted his cheek.

"Come back, son. Please don't leave me." She squeezed his hand and called for his father. As Conall opened his eyes, his mother peppered him with kisses, shouting praises through prayer that her son had been saved.

His father stumbled in his haste to climb down the stairs. The panic in his eyes turned to amazement when he saw his son. "You're alive."

Leana's eyes glistened with tears as she watched the parents' joyful reunion with their son. She turned to leave, exhausted from giving him part of herself.

"You." Conall's voice broke through the voices.

Leana jerked around and met his gaze. She'd forgotten that while everyone else would be oblivious to her presence, he'd be able to see her. Her eyes grew wide. Would he give her away? Or worse, reject her again?

"Thank you." He smiled, ignoring the looks of confusion from his parents as they glanced up to see who he was talking to.

She nodded before disappearing through the door. It was time to leave and let them celebrate. If he wanted to see her, he would find her later. Exhaustion like she'd never known threatened to overpower her as she made her way to the barrows.

Fiona's home was still empty months after her death, and Leana welcomed the silence. Most of the furniture had been taken or sold, but there was still the old mattress Fiona slept on. Leana dropped, curled up in a ball, hoping sleep would overtake her.

She had nearly drifted off when searing pain shot through her. It was a hunger pang, but more severe than she'd felt before. After as many souls as she'd had lately, simply giving Conall part of her should not have affected her like this. But then, she'd never allowed herself to get so close to a victim before.

CHAPTER FIFTEEN

CONALL

Conall brushed Aengus's mane, whistling to himself. He felt better than he had since before he left, and while he wanted to get back to investigating the rise in deaths, his father advised him to continue resting.

From what he could gather, the couple had found him on the ground and instantly called for help. They'd shipped him back as soon as they could. It was quite a surprise for him to wake up in his own house with Leana standing near him. Her beautiful face framed by that wild red hair had shown relief as their eyes met.

He couldn't get her out of his mind, no matter what he tried. Once he'd realized that leaving her to go to another country had only made his longing for her worse, he decided to embrace it and finally admit his feelings for her.

Da had made Conall promise that he wouldn't go hunting, but he'd said nothing about going to find Leana.

"Ready?" Conall climbed up and patted Aengus's neck. "Find her."

Aengus started at a slow trot, then turned to the west and broke into a gallop. Conall grinned as the miles swept by. He had no idea how Aengus knew where he was going, but he wasn't going to question it.

They stopped a couple of hours in so that Aengus could rest and they could both eat. Conall stared off in the distance, feeling Leana closer to him. He wondered again about the connection between them. He had no idea what had caused it, but he knew it had only grown stronger after she'd saved his life.

It was nearing sunset when they reached the coast. He could feel her near, but it still took another hour before he finally saw her. He grinned and nearly called out when he saw a tear run down her cheek. Was it because of him? Or was it something else? He stood mesmerized by her beauty. Her red hair flowed out behind her, showing off her long, slim neck. Aengus nudged him forward and Conall took a step, knowing that he would do whatever it took to wash away her pain.

CHAPTER SIXTEEN

LEANA

The investigations into the mysterious deaths were well underway, which meant Leana had to avoid any of the gathering places for music or galleries. She was starving, and while she'd tried to inspire other men to produce masterpieces, their spirits just simply faded away into nothing.

She stared out at the sunset on the coast. It was a solitary place, which is what she needed at the moment. Conall was somewhere near. She could feel his closeness like her own heartbeat. While she wouldn't allow him to see her, she knew that being apart would only kill him faster.

"Hello, Leana." Conall's voice washed over her like a warm blanket.

She didn't turn, though she wanted to run into his arms. Conall sat next to her and dangled his feet over the edge.

"You weren't supposed to know I was here." Her

voice was monotone, lacking her usual flirtatious undertones. She couldn't make herself use her powers on him. She cared too much for him.

His shoulder bumped her. "I always know where you are. I'm not sure why, but it comes in handy when I want to find you."

"Maybe it's just my beauty and glowing personality." She laughed, though she didn't feel the humor.

He joined in. "I'm sure that's it."

"Where were you?" Leana asked. "You left me. Where did you go?"

"I went to Scotland for a job. Da asked me to, and since I had nothing keeping me here, I decided to go." Conall glanced down at her.

Leana ducked her head. She'd hurt him and deserved that guilt that he'd laid on her shoulders. "How was Scotland?"

She'd heard of the place—there were supposedly others like her—but it was a place she'd never see. She belonged here on the Emerald Isle.

"It was beautiful. The mountains, the lochs, the architecture in the city. I loved it all. But I didn't see as much of the land as I'd hoped I would."

"What do you mean?" She cocked her head. "You were gone for months."

Conall stared down at his hands. "I helped the crew for the cost of the trip, and they were appreciative because of my size. It was when Ireland was on the horizon that I fell ill. I pushed it off, believing it was seasickness. But it only got worse once we landed in Scotland."

Leana frowned. "What do you mean?"

"I was able to work, but only for short periods of time. It was as though there a vice squeezing my chest. I had high hopes of painting the buildings I'd only read about before, but I was so sick, I never even got out my paints. When I returned to Ireland, I had to be put in a wagon and brought to my parents that way. I was ready to see my Maker. I had a good family, lived the best life I could, and while she wouldn't have me, I had the woman of my dreams. I was ready to go."

"I felt you come home."

He took Leana's hand and kissed it. "And I felt you as well. Your kiss brought me back to life." He laughed. "Me parents are convinced it was an angel, and since no one else could see you, I wondered if they were right." His eyes searched Leana's. "Is that what you are? An angel?"

"I . . . suppose I am." An angel of death. One who stole life from innocent men. One who needed his life force to survive, but she would rather die than take it. "And as much as I want to be with you, we can never be together."

Conall nodded. "I know. But I also don't want to live without you. I *can't* live without you. I don't plan on going anywhere. Not anymore."

Leana smiled. If she could just take the smallest amount of his life force from him . . . but no. She'd already accidentally killed Fiona that way. "I'd like to know that you'll always be there for me. I haven't had that before."

He tipped her chin and kissed her, and while she tried to hold back, her emotions flowed through her. She wouldn't let his soul leave him, as much as it wanted to be part of her. When she couldn't take the flood anymore, she pulled away and stood.

She wanted to flee again, but she forced herself to stay. "Shall we walk?"

Conall stood, and they walked down the path toward a small village. He bought the two of them some mincemeat pies and told her stories from his time on the ship. Leana did her best to avoid touching him, for fear that she would release her essence and pull on his soul again. It was right there, just begging to be taken.

"Hey, look. There's a puppet show. We should go." Conall pointed toward a small building.

"Puppets?" She stood back from the entrance. She wasn't sure it was a good idea to be around people in such an enclosed space.

"Don't tell me you've never seen a puppet show before. Come on." He pulled her inside and purchased two tickets for the show.

The lights went down in the theater, and the actors

began the show. They told the stories of Cu Chulainn, adding humor in the midst of the tragedy. Leana was mesmerized by the small puppets. How did they make them work? It wasn't magic or she would have felt it.

When it ended she was the first to jump up and clap, eager to find out what was behind the puppet stage. Conall grabbed her hand as she headed for the stage.

"Whoa, where are you going?"

"I must see these puppets." She tried to pull away, but he held tighter.

"You've really never seen a puppet show before?" he asked.

Was that bad? She looked around and others were leaving, not amazed at all by what had just happened on the stage.

"No, but I want to see more. When can we watch the next one?" Leana stared at the stage, waiting for the puppets to start up again.

Conall shook his head and led her to the front of the room. "One moment."

Leana waited as Conall spoke to someone behind the stage. A moment later, two men came out wearing the puppets on their hands. Leana gasped and leaned forward to inspect them, yanking one off the guy's hand. "Why, they're not real at all. They're just . . . dolls."

The men laughed as Conall apologized and shook their hands before leaving the building. As soon as they were around the corner, he pulled Leana into a hug, then kissed her soundly.

Leana stepped away, dazed. "What was that for?"

"I love your view of life. It's so . . . innocent. And refreshing." He kissed her again, having no idea what kind of battle warred within her each time he came near. When they finally broke apart, he took her hand and walked down the path away from the village.

Leana stayed silent. Innocent was something she was not. Naive to the things of the human world, yes. But not innocent.

"Are you hungry? Should we eat somewhere?" His lighthearted demeanor contrasted sharply with the dark shadow over Leana's own heart.

She wanted to say no, to end the evening right there. Being around him was too much, but the thought of leaving him sent her to a dark place. "I could go for a drink."

"Perfect. I know this little pub just down the road from here. It serves the best cottage pie and ale in Ireland."

The mention of cottage pie shook her. She hadn't eaten it since the night Fiona died. She assured herself that she wouldn't have to eat it. She listened as Conall told her a story of visiting here with his brothers, and she hoped that he wouldn't notice that she wasn't participating in the conversation. She loved his stories. She'd known many poets and writers over the years that couldn't tell a story nearly as well as he could. But she could never push him to write them down. Not if it meant eventual death for him.

"Ah, here we are. It doesn't look like much, but trust me, you'll love it." He opened the door for her, then led her up to the bar, keeping his hand on the small of her back. He ordered food for himself, and she settled on fish and chips when he insisted. Once he'd paid, they found a table in the back of the pub.

"So, you've made me talk the whole time. I want to know about you. You told me da that you were from the barrows, but there are barrows all over Ireland." He gave her his full attention, making her nervous.

"We moved all over. My . . . family doesn't sit still for long." Family. Fiona counted as family. As did the Leanan Sidhe that came before her.

He nodded. "I've seen that just from trying to keep up with you. Did any of your family ever settle down into one place?"

"Me aunt did. The one who I helped at the market."

The lying was becoming easier, but she wondered if he actually believed her.

"Ah, yes. Your aunt. The reason we met." He leaned back in his chair and smiled. "How is she doing?"

Leana's face dropped. "She's dead."

Conall gripped her hand tightly. "My condolences. How long ago?"

"The night I met you. The trip back home was too much for her." It didn't matter what the banshee had said. She couldn't be the reason for Fiona dying.

"Why didn't you tell me?" Conall scooted his chair closer, as if his closeness would wash away the pain.

Leana shrugged. "You never asked."

"I don't suppose I did. But I still wish you'd said something." Conall moved so the waitress could put the food on their table. "You're not used to sharing things with people, are you?"

Leana nearly choked on her chip. She shared inspiration with anyone she came in contact with. But no, that wasn't what he meant. "No. I like being on my own. Well, I did. Not anymore."

"I was the same way." He smiled and picked up his fork. "This cottage pie smells so good. I've been waiting a long time for it."

Leana watched as he took a bite. She could almost

taste it, just like Fiona had made. It was a little bland compared to other foods she'd been forced to eat, but she still ate it to keep up her strength. She ate a small piece of her fish, regretting that she hadn't ordered what he had.

"Would you like a bite?" He pushed his dish a little closer.

"But it's your food." Leana cocked her head to the side. "Why would you share it?"

Conall chuckled. "Because you were looking at it like you wanted some."

"So you would just give it to me?" Leana shook her head. Humans were so strange.

"Not all of it." He took her fork, scooped up some of the pie, and handed it to her.

Leana took the fork from him and tried it. The flavors burst in her mouth, a perfect blend of spices, meat, and vegetables. It was hot and burnt her tongue, but all she could think about was having another bite. "I've never tasted anything like it. My aunt's pie was the only cottage pie I've had, and it tasted like nothing."

"Take another bite if you'd like." He took one of the chips off her plate. "Do you mind?"

"If you're sharing yours, 'tis only fair for me to share

mine." She had another bite of the pie, no longer wanting the fish and chips. This night just kept getting better, and she was able to forget the sorrow of knowing that one day Conall would no longer be around.

CHAPTER SEVENTEEN

CONALL

C onall lay in bed the next morning, thinking over the time he'd spent with Leana. It had been the perfect night, and he'd hated to see it end. She'd gone back to wherever it was that she lived, and he could already feel the ache of not having her near.

He knew he needed to get up. A message had been waiting for him when he'd returned home. They'd found another dead composer the day before, and this time it was in Cork. It was a relief to know that it was so far away from where he'd run into Leana last night. It couldn't have been her.

The thought that there could be a copycat crossed his mind, but it was impossible for anyone else to do whatever this creature had done. From the description, he was found on his couch, and while he used to be overweight, it appeared as though he had shrunk almost to nothing.

Whatever it was needed to be stopped. Conall

climbed out of bed and changed into his clothes. Mam had made food, so he stopped long enough to eat before going out to saddle Aengus.

The trip was long enough that Conall had Aengus cross through forests so they could get there faster. He wanted to investigate the scene and get back up to meet Leana. There was a concert in the village two days from now and she was insistent that she wanted to go.

Wind howled through the trees as he avoided the oncoming storm as much as possible. Perhaps he should have sent someone who was closer. He wasn't the only one on the case, but he'd seen more of the victims than the others.

Rain poured down on him for the last few miles. He rode Aengus into the nearest stable and made sure he was taken care of before running into the home. He was soaked to the bone, but he wanted to get the investigation over with. He took off his coat so it wouldn't make a mess in the room, and followed the inspector into the front room.

Fingerprint powder was all over everything, but otherwise, the room was untouched. The man lay where he died. Conall had to cover his mouth and nose as he got closer because of how long they'd left him there.

He did look like the others, although he seemed more pale. Conall bent closer to check the man's neck. He cursed under his breath. This wasn't a copycat case, but it also wasn't the creature who had attacked before.

"We have a vampire." He pointed out the marks on the man's neck. "Have you heard of any more victims in the area?"

"No, sir. But are you sure it's not the same thing?" A short, stocky man stood nearby taking notes.

Conall pursed his lips. "Yes. I'm sure. The others didn't have bites like this man. Now, if I were you, I would collect all the garlic and wooden stakes you can find." He pulled his soaked coat back on. "Unless there's something else, I'm going to head back home before I wash away."

The man followed him to the door. "But sir. You don't want to go out there in this. You'll never make it home. Besides, we were told you would stop the creature. What difference does it make if it's a vampire and not something else? Either way, we're losing people."

The rain that had been bad before was now flooding the streets. Conall closed the door and turned. He wouldn't be leaving anytime soon. "Okay, let's search the room to see if there's any other clues that we've been missing. I went through the other victims' homes thoroughly, but the only odd thing I could find was that their music or art had disappeared. That's not the case here."

The man looked at him strangely. "What do you mean? Why would their music just disappear?"

"Most of it has turned up on a castle step or music hall. Always with a note stating their name and the name of the piece." Conall crouched down next to a pile of papers. "See this? All of his music's still here. And look, there's some blood."

Once they were busy studying every inch of the room, Conall checked the weather outside. He could already feel the effects of being so far away from Leana. He needed to get back or he'd collapse again. But how was he supposed to tell anyone else that?

The rain still came down in thick sheets. It would be hard on Aengus if they tried to leave right now.

"Sir?" A voice said from behind him.

"Yes?" Conall followed the small man back into the living room.

The group stared down at a paper on the floor. Blood had spattered across it, but that's not what was unique. The man had written the word *Dearg Due* on the paper. It was mostly likely the last thing he'd written.

"Is that possible? This is too far south for her. And that's only if she could escape from her grave." The stocky man wrung his hands. Dearg Due was a vampire, but she'd supposedly been trapped decades before.

"Strange deaths are happening throughout the country and you wonder how she could get free?" Conall closed his eyes, running through the other scenes, but they were just too different from this. "Tomorrow, you need to make sure that someone heads to her burial site and places more stones on her grave. Hopefully she won't be able to get out again. If that doesn't work, you'll have to have a few people sleep near there and have their stakes at the ready in case she escapes."

Conall glanced at the window again. "Does anyone know of a place I can stay tonight? I won't be going anywhere for a while."

"There's an inn just up the road." The stocky man held out his hand to shake. "It was a pleasure to meet you. I will be sure to keep in touch."

"Thank you." Conall left and ran up the block to the inn. His clothes were soaked through and left a trail of water on the floor as he walked through to the office. He smiled at the man standing behind the counter. "Hello, I need a room for the night."

The man had him sign a book and then handed him the keys. "Go upstairs and down the hall. Bathroom is right next to it. Dinner is in an hour."

Conall headed up the stairs to his room, glancing back to see a maid mopping up the mess he'd made. Once in his room, he pulled off his shoes and jacket so he could dry off, wishing he'd thought of bringing an extra change of clothes.

The rain had stopped sometime during the night, leaving large puddles throughout the town. Conall finished his breakfast and thanked the innkeeper's wife for her hospitality. He noticed his coat was still damp on his way to get Aengus, but there wasn't anything he could do about it.

The evidence of having Dearg Due free shed a new light on the case, and Conall was eager to find out if there was a connection to the other cases. As much as he wanted to believe they were closer to solving them, he was sure it was two different creatures, and he didn't like knowing he'd taken a step backward.

The trip back home was much slower because they had to watch for slick mud and puddles that were deeper than they seemed. As the hours passed by, the weakness and pressure Conall had felt in Scotland became stronger, and he knew he needed to find Leana as soon as possible. Relief filled him as the village came into view near sunset. He dropped Aengus off at a stable and followed Leana's directions to the theater where the concert was to take place.

An orchestra sat on stage ready to perform as he slipped in through the door. He searched the crowd and smiled when he found Leana's red hair. He excused himself as he scooted in through the row to sit next to her.

"Sorry I'm late."

Her face brightened. "I'd thought you'd forgotten."

"No, I would never miss it. I got stuck while I was on a job and couldn't get back up here." He put his arm around her, enjoying how she snuggled in, laying her head against his shoulder. As they sat listening to the music, his energy slowly returned. He kissed the top of her head, happy to have him back with her. "You never told me who is performing tonight."

Leana stiffened slightly. "It's a new composer. You wouldn't recognize his name."

"He's very good. It's too bad he didn't get to hear it for himself." Conall let the comment slip without realizing what he'd said. Leana didn't respond but the look of pride on her face saddened him. It was possible that he would already know the name of the composer through his investigations. He just hoped he was wrong.

Leana tapped her foot in rhythm as the concert continued and when it ended, she stood and cheered with the rest of the crowd. "They did a wonderful job with the music. I especially liked that last song."

"They really did." Conall led her out of the concert hall. "Should we go to my place for dinner? Mam is probably expecting me after being gone since yesterday morning."

"I would love to see your farm again." She smiled, though her eyes seemed more tired than usual.

"Let me get Aengus." Conall went to the stables and made sure the saddle was tight before going to find Leana. She stood near the main street watching the people as they walked by. "Here we go."

He helped her up and then climbed up behind her.

She leaned into him as they traveled, and he was content not to say anything as they galloped across the valley. The sun had set long before, and Conall began to grow uneasy. Something was out there that he didn't like.

"Hold tight. There are dark things that roam the night." He nudged Aengus with his foot to urge the horse to go faster.

"What do you mean?" Her voice was sleepy as she snuggled up closer to him.

Conall stayed silent for a moment. "Well, there are wolves and other creatures out there. Tonight seems to be . . . off. I'd rather not be out right now."

"I think you're right." Leana yawned and snuggled closer.

"If you'd like, I can have my mam whip up a cottage pie. Hers compares to the one you had the other night." Conall pushed her hair out of his face.

Leana nodded. "I have to admit that I've craved that ever since I had some of yours. But if it's too much to ask, I won't worry about it. We can eat whatever she's already made."

"Mam has a hard time sleeping on some nights, so she'll be happy to have something to do. It'll be just fine." Conall nudged Aengus again, this time allowing him to break into a full gallop. He could feel Leana leaning heavier against him, and he guessed she was falling asleep in his arms.

The stables soon appeared at the bottom of the hill. Once they'd stopped, he climbed down and then helped Leana. She nearly collapsed as she stood, and Conall had to pick her up.

"Are you okay?" he asked.

She nodded. "I just haven't eaten for a while, and I need more energy as soon as possible."

"I'll get you taken care of right now." He hurried into the house and laid her on the couch. "Mam?"

It was a few minutes before Mam came from the bedroom tying her robe. "What kept you? I was expecting you hours ago."

"A storm, and then I attended a concert with her. Did you happen to save any dinner?"

Mam walked to the oven and pulled out a large casserole. "It should still be warm."

"Thanks, Mam." Conall knelt next to the couch. "Leana? Dinner is ready. Can you sit up? Leana?"

She didn't move. Her pulse barely registered under his fingers, and her chest barely rose with her breathing. Conall shook her, but her eyes remained closed.

"What happened to her?" Mam rushed to Conall's side.

"I don't know, but she needs help. Can you fetch the doctor?" Conall didn't want to move, worried that being apart from her would only make it worse. He waited for Mam to leave the house and hoped Da wouldn't come in. He leaned forward, kissing her lightly, hoping that it would help her. If she was what he thought, she needed to feed off a soul, and he wasn't about to let her take his mam's.

A small gasp rose from her lips, and Conall pulled away. He watched as her breathing became regular, and she stirred slightly. He ran his fingers through his hair as he backed away and went into the kitchen. It was possible that the kiss alone was enough to jerk her back, but the way he suddenly felt drained of energy told him otherwise. She was right. It *was* too dangerous to be around her. He knew what she was, and it was a death sentence for both of them.

CHAPTER EIGHTEEN

LEANA

Dreams plagued Leana as she tried to pull herself out of the sleep she was stuck inside. Somewhere she'd gained the energy to survive, and she needed to use it to feed again. Had Conall tried to resuscitate her? Maybe. He was a human after all, and they didn't seem to know when to let Death take their families from them.

Slowly she forced her eyelids open. This was the weakest she'd ever allowed herself to become, but she couldn't afford to take the souls from the people as they watched the concert for fear that she would take too much of Conall's because of their connection. She should never have invited him.

The banging of pots and pans came through her reverie and she turned her head to find Conall in his kitchen. His hair fell into his eyes just perfectly. Every ounce of her ached to take his soul right then and there, but she couldn't. And she hated it.

"Conall?" Her voice was barely over a whisper as she tried to sit up.

He rushed over to her side and pulled her up. "You had me worried. What happened?"

She shook her head. "I don't know. I must be hungrier than I thought."

"I have dinner for you." He smiled and helped her to the table. "Mam made casserole. It's close to cottage pie, so I hope you like it."

Leana smiled. "I'm sure I will. Thank you."

Conall watched her take a bite before taking one of his own. "She went to go find a doctor. I guess you don't need one anymore."

"No, I'm fine now." Leana watched as Conall picked at his food. "Is there something wrong?"

"What? No. I—you really scared me." He smiled weakly and clasped her hand. "Maybe I shouldn't have dragged you all the way here to eat. The pub in town would have done just fine."

He had no idea how right he was. Here she would have to go after one of his neighbors, and she hated the thought. Maybe if she took some of the life source from their animals, it would allow her to get back into town. She shuddered.

"You don't like the food?" Conall's voice interrupted her thoughts.

"What? No. I mean, I love it. Your mam is a wonderful cook. I was just . . . thinking of the nightmares I had before waking." She took another bite to show him how much she enjoyed it, but inside she was still nauseated at the thought of taking the spirits of animals. "I do need to leave soon, though."

Conall frowned, but nodded. "I understand. Maybe we can see each other tomorrow?"

"I would love that very much." Leana stared down at her empty plate. If anything, it had only made her hunger worse.

"Would you like more?"

"I don't want to eat all of your food. Your mam obviously worked very hard to make this."

Conall put another two servings on her plate. "Mam doesn't like food to go to waste. With my brothers out of the house, she finds herself making too much, and she'll be happy to know that it's been eaten."

"Well, I'm glad I can help then." Leana finished what was on her plate and was on her third helping when Conall's mother returned.

An older man came in behind her, carrying a medical bag. He studied Leana with narrowed eyes, but said nothing as Conall's mother introduced them to each other. He seemed vaguely familiar to Leana, but she couldn't place where she knew him from.

"You look like you're doing much better." He pulled out his stethoscope.

"Yes, I am, thank you." Leana glanced between the three humans in front of her. What was she supposed to do? The food had helped give her energy, but it would wear out quickly.

Conall watched as the doctor checked her eyes, pulse, and lungs, then stood to help his mother clean up dinner. Even then, Leana could tell that Conall was listening to everything that passed between her and the doctor.

"Well, she seems fine now. If there's nothing else you need, I'll get back to my bed." He set his stethoscope in his bag and limped over to the door.

Leana jumped up, knowing if she didn't leave soon, she wouldn't be able to leave at all. "Thank you again for dinner. I must be getting home."

Conall took a step forward. "I can take you."

"Thank you, but I will be fine. I have family in the next village over, and I can stay with them." It was a total lie, and she was sure Conall knew that too.

"Very well." He pulled her into a hug and kissed her. "Be careful out there. I worry about what's in the woods tonight. You know, maybe I should go with you."

Leana kissed him to stop the flow of words. "I will be fine. I promise."

With one more goodbye to his mother, she left the house and jumped when she saw the doctor standing there silently. She turned to leave, but he grabbed her arm.

"I know what you are." His grip was strong as he pulled her to him. "I need you."

"I don't know what you're talking about." Leana tried to pull away.

"You look the same as you did over sixty years ago. I was so jealous of him when he caught your attention. But then I saw what you did to him. It was a secret I kept even as I saw his brother marry and as his wife bore a son. When I found you at the table tonight . . ." His eyes stared off into the darkness as he went back to that time. "Please. Do the same thing for me."

Leana jerked back, her mind reeling. "You knew him?"

"Aye. We were friends since we were lads. And now I am ready to be laid to rest as he was. Please. I lost my wife last year, and I can't go on without her." The pain in his voice nearly broke her.

"I can't just . . . if I took your life, Conall and his mam would be suspicious." Leana rubbed her forehead. She needed the life force. But was she willing to take this man's life?

The man laughed as he limped toward his carriage, still holding onto Leana's wrist. "No one will check on me for days. I have no one left who cares for me."

Leana glanced back at Conall's house before climbing in the carriage beside the old man. They were several miles from the farmhouse when she took the last few breaths from him. He deserved more of a memorial than he would have gotten if she'd killed him at home. She untied one of the horses, cut almost all the way through the rope on the other horse, then slapped the horse's rump so the carriage would go flying as the horse went around a corner. This way his death would seem like an accident.

She climbed up on the horse and rode back to the village. While the man had brought her some much-needed energy, she would need to feed again soon.

It was another three days before Leana finally found a story about the doctor in the paper. She smiled in satisfaction when they mentioned the tragic accident. His wife was mentioned, as was a son she didn't know he'd had.

Conall hadn't been around much over the last few days, always saying he had a job to do. Anger and sadness burned through her, and the surrounding villages seemed to suffer from it.

She climbed on the horse she'd taken from the doctor and made her way back to Carman's cave. This time she blew the door open, not waiting for the old witch to answer it.

"I see you've forgotten your manners since you were here last." The old woman chuckled and dumped the contents from her mortar into a small bottle. "How may I help you?"

"Nothing is working. I tried to stay away from him,

and I nearly died. He left me, and he nearly died. I tried to use the emotions like you wanted me to, but the only thing that's happened is that I hurt more when I refuse to take his soul."

Carman was silent as she continued to grind more herbs. The continuous motion only fed Leana's temper until she was ready to throw the herbs across the room.

"Why are you here?"

"Because—it seems that I made a mistake in freeing a few other spirits from their prisons. I can't flee anywhere now without fear that Dearg Due has already caused enough commotion that I can no longer feed for fear of being caught. I need your help trapping her." Leana picked up one of the vials on Carman's table and made a face. Herbs. Such a waste of time.

Carman set down the pestle and met Leana's eyes. "She must be destroyed, and only the hunters can do that. Perhaps it's time for you to go to sleep until all this has all passed."

"Perhaps . . . but what about Conall? It would kill him." Leana dropped into a chair and buried her face in her hands.

"It seems to me that this has nothing to do with Dearg Due or any other spirit you've released. You need to decide if you care more for his life or for yours. And it's only *you* who can decide that. Now, leave me. Your petulance is tiresome." Carman went back to grinding herbs, ignoring Leana, who sat there staring at her in shock.

Petulant? Leana huffed and stormed outside. Maybe she was, but for good reason. She should never have released the vampire. But now it was time to rectify her mistake. Leana wanted Conall for herself, but until the vampire was gone, no one in this land was safe. She would lead the hunter straight to Dearg Due and be rid of her once and for all.

CHAPTER NINETEEN
CONALL

The country was in an uproar, and Conall was at the heart of it. While his dad still hunted, it was Conall who people turned to when there was a vicious spirit nearby. People were afraid to leave their houses even during the daytime for fear that their loved ones would pass away while they were gone.

Conall ached to have Leana near him, but at this point it wasn't wise to spend time with her. Not while other hunters were looking for her. He watched out the window of the small pub, wishing she was with him. Even the cottage pie wasn't enough to cheer him up.

He threw money on the table and shoved his hat down far enough to nearly cover his eyes. There was to be a meeting with a few other hunters, but no one had shown. He left the pub and glanced around before going to the stable to find Aengus.

After making a quick inspection to make sure it was indeed his horse—kelpies had tried too often lately to impersonate him—he climbed on and rode back toward home. Chances are he would hear of his companions' deaths in the newspaper soon enough.

As they rode down the pathway, Conall pulled out his notebook and sketched Leana's face for the hundredth time. It was the way he helped keep her near him. It wasn't until the rider was nearly upon him that Conall jerked his head up to see him.

"Conall? I was told to send for you immediately." The man's brown hair stood on end from riding without a hat. His eyes were wild. "We found her. Or at least we think we did."

Conall watched as the man whipped his horse around and fly back the way he'd come from. Aengus jolted forward to catch up to the other rider. They'd searched for Dearg Due for weeks, but she continued to elude them. The deaths had become more violent than the first man Conall had seen in Cork, and he dreaded what he would see when he got there.

"The neighbors heard screams coming from the house earlier tonight and sent for help immediately. This is the third attack in three days, and we can only assume she'll hit again tonight." The constable pointed out several houses on a crudely drawn map. "She has to be hiding out nearby because she's attacking specific homes."

Conall nodded and looked through the information for the other cases. "Where are the homes?"

The constable and assistants exchanged glances. "You don't want to go inside."

"I need to know what happened there. Where are the homes?" Conall swallowed hard, knowing it was a bad idea, but he had to know.

"Denis will take you to see them." The constable gestured toward the door. The man who had come to find Conall left, waiting for Conall to follow him.

"Did you know it was this bad?" Conall asked.

"No. I only knew of the attack tonight." Denis climbed on his horse and they moved through the center of town.

The eerie silence weighed heavily on Conall. The streets should have still been full of people going about their last-minute errands. The houses were lit, but no one was visible. They were most likely holed up inside, hoping they weren't next.

Three houses stood at the end of the street, darkened. The doors were broken off their hinges. Conall climbed down and handed the reins to Denis when it was clear he wasn't going in.

A lantern sat just inside the door along with some matches. Conall lit it and made his way inside, covering his nose and mouth. Papers and broken furniture were scattered throughout the house, along with what looked like blood. Conall's stomach knotted, but he knew he needed to see where the family had died.

Moments later he burst out of the house and dropped to the ground retching. Denis handed him a handkerchief, but said nothing as Conall tried to compose himself. Once he could stand, he took the top of the lantern off and threw it into the house, allowing it to catch fire. He nodded toward the next house, and Denis did the same to that one. They took a burning rug from the second house and threw it into the last before heading back to the station.

Conall was willing to plan their next steps, but he refused to speak of what he'd seen inside the house, even though he knew it would continue to haunt his dreams forever.

"And you're sure she comes before sunset?" Conall stared down at the logistics of their plan.

"Aye. At least that's what she's done every night leading up to this." Denis put a third wooden stake into his belt, ready to fight.

Conall rubbed his chin. "But why not after nightfall? It makes no sense."

"It's how the curse was set." Leana's voice interrupted them from the doorway. "Sorry, I was told you were here."

"Leana, I thought we were meeting later." Conall swept her up in his arms.

She laughed and pulled away. "I wanted to surprise you. I hope you don't mind."

"Of course not." Except that he wanted her nowhere near here. It was too dangerous. "What do you mean about the curse?"

"When she was locked into her grave, they cursed it so she would be locked in at night, thinking that's when she would attack. Somehow she must have found her way around the curse, attacking just before the curse sets in." Leana pursed her lips, an angry blush creeping up her face.

Conall studied her for a moment before turning back to the others. "You heard that, people. We only have a few moments to get her before she's trapped for another day. I don't want to have to burn down another house, so we must stop her tonight."

The group of hunters left to take their positions, leaving Conall and Leana alone. He looked down at her and caressed her cheek.

"I'm sorry I've been gone so much. I've missed you." He kissed her and pulled her into a hug.

"I don't understand why you're here. You were supposed to be working on your farm. When I asked your da, he didn't want to tell me where you'd gone." She snuggled closer.

Conall froze. Had she done something to Da? "How'd you get him to tell you?"

She chuckled. "I do what any woman does when she wants something. I cried."

"Ah. That will get Da to do just about anything." Conall laughed with her, relief spreading through him.

"That doesn't answer my question, though. Why are you here?"

Conall hesitated. She knew of the hunters. What would she think of him being one? "I knew they needed help, so I volunteered."

She pulled away, fear etched in her beautiful features. "I don't want you here. Come away with me."

"I can't leave. I need to help them stop this." He kissed her again and pulled away. "I hope you understand."

Leana's face changed from fear to anger as she took a step back. "You cannot be here. Death will come and I won't allow it."

Anger surged through him. "Leana, I love you, but I cannot just leave these people to die. I will meet you when this is done."

"Don't bother." Her icy glare burned into him, then she stormed out and slammed the door.

Conall ducked his head, pain shooting through him. It was as if the connection to her had been severed, leaving him breathless.

Shouts echoed through the square, knocking him into action. He could mourn later. Conall sprinted out of the building and down the street to where the crowd had gathered. Shattering glass came from inside the house, followed by screaming. Conall continued past the men who stood frozen in place by fear and stepped over the broken-down door. He had no idea how the vampire had managed to get inside when people were standing watch, but he had to be ready for anything.

The rooms downstairs remained quiet, so Conall crept up the steps, holding his stake out behind him. His other hand rested on his father's pistol, loaded with bullets they'd gotten blessed by a local priest. Noise rustled in the room on his right. Conall took a deep breath and pushed the door opened to find a beautiful, frightening young woman. Her hair was long and golden, and her eyes captivated him. If it weren't for the white fangs framed by her scowl, he would have fallen for her with every ounce of his being.

She hissed and stood, ignoring the man she'd left lying on the ground. Her countenance instantly changed from one of anger to a flirtatious smile. "Well, hello. Aren't you handsome?"

Conall's skin crawled as she came near him, running her hands along his chest, licking her lips. He kept his hand holding the stake behind him, hoping she wouldn't see it. "I'd heard if I waited just long enough, that I would find the most beautiful woman that has ever graced the earth. I guess my soothsayer was right."

Dearg Due purred as she moved in closer. "I think

I'll keep you as a pet. Hold on while I finish what I was doing."

The man on the floor whimpered, earning a hiss from her.

"Forget him. He's no man." Conall took his hand from the pistol and pulled her close.

"Oh, I like you." Her fangs became longer as she went for his neck, but Conall was quicker.

The stake went through her heart from the back and barely missed Conall's chest. She stared down in shock and staggered backward, trying to grab for it. Conall quickly followed with the pistol. As soon as the shots went off, she fell to the ground.

"Get out of here. Now," Conall yelled to the man. He quickly bound the vampire with cords soaked in garlic. Adrenaline coursed through his body as he dragged her down the stairs.

Footsteps thundered into the house, and several men helped lift her body and take it outside. Conall stood on the porch as the townspeople went through the rituals to ensure that she would never rise again.

As soon as he could trust himself to stand, he stumbled over to the station where Aengus waited for him and climbed up. "Take me home."

It would take several showers to wash the darkness off of him. And even then, Conall wasn't sure he would be the same.

CHAPTER TWENTY

LEANA

Leana fled to the north as far away from Conall as she could get. How dare he disobey her? She'd warned him to stay away from the vampire, and he hadn't listened. Shock, anger, and overwhelming depression shook her.

Conall had been lying about why he was there in that office. He was supposed to be a starving artist. He was supposed to be *her* artist. Clearly, that was not the case. There was something more to him that he wasn't telling her. And in that, Leana felt a strange kind of freedom. She could go after someone else now.

She made her way to the university in Cork, figuring she would find an artist there who would appreciate her. Many of the people were already in bed, but others would be studying. The art school was filled with students making sculptures or painting. She smiled to herself as she went from one student to the next, sharing her inspiration, while taking a little of their essence in the process.

Perhaps instead of hibernating, she would stay here. As long as she didn't choose one person in particular, she could live off the students for another few decades at least. As long as she didn't take too much from any of them, no one would suspect that she was here.

CHAPTER TWENTY-ONE

CONALL

Leana had disappeared completely. Conall had searched for her over the last few months, but he could no longer feel her. He should have been glad that she was no longer in his life. The attacks had stopped when she left, which should have also made him happy. Instead, he ached for her even more.

After the encounter with the vampire, Conall had fled to Scotland. This time he didn't have the same crushing pain he'd had before. And if he really wanted to be honest, he'd only left to prove that he could.

He folded the worn letter from Da and shoved it back into his coat as he stared out at the Irish coastline. Mam had grown ill suddenly and passed away a fortnight before. Da had wanted to wait until Conall could get there for the funeral, but he knew that the letter wouldn't reach him in time.

The deckhands shouted to each other as they readied the ship to dock in Dublin. Conall pushed past the other families who were leaving the ship and ran for the nearest stables. When he couldn't find a suitable horse, he hired out a buggy.

He set his things inside the buggy, then held out a bag of coins. "There's another one of these if you can get me home by sunset."

The driver's eyes grew large and he nodded, tucking the money in his coat.

Conall climbed in and closed the door behind him. It was another few minutes before they could leave, but then the driver broke through onto the empty road. The landscape flew past him, but not fast enough. He should have been there. Mam had taken such good care of him, and now she was gone.

The driver pulled away from the farmhouse, leaving Conall staring out at the farm. He walked inside to find Da sitting at the table. He looked up when Conall came in, but said nothing. It was if he'd aged decades since Conall had last seen him.

Conall sat next to him. "I wish I was here."

"The wake was beautiful. But it doesn't bring her back." Da rubbed his eyes. "I miss her, son."

"I know, Da." He took the dishes and set them in the sink. "Where are Gael and Edmond?"

"They returned to school yesterday. I was supposed to tell you hello from them."

Conall returned to the table. "I have the rest of my luggage coming. I'm moving back home to help you out with the farm."

Da smiled. "I'd like that. But I think I'm going to sell the land. There's too much for me to handle."

"But this land has been in our family for generations." Conall felt like the wind had been knocked out of him. "I thought Gael had planned to farm it. He's talked about it for years."

"Aye, but his wife would have nothing to do with the life of a farmer's wife. When you left, he moved off to Dublin and went to work for her family."

Why hadn't he heard anything about this while he was gone? Da had written to him several times and never brought it up. "Let me buy it."

Da shook his head. "I can't let you do that. You're needed out there. You're ten times the hunter I ever was and the country—or the world—needs you."

"And I can do that from here." Conall dropped the coins and bills he'd saved over the last few months onto the table. "That's a deposit. I'll pay the rest as I get it."

Da stared at the money, not speaking for several moments. Finally, he gathered it and held it back out. "The land is yours. Save the money. You'll need it later. I'll have our lender draw up the papers to turn the farm over to you."

Conall should have known that the quiet farm life wasn't meant for him. Da continued to work by his side,

119

but he wasn't the same since Mam died. He no longer hunted, leaving all of that life to Conall as well.

It was late one night that Conall heard a pounding on the door. He jumped out of his bed and grabbed his crossbow, knowing what it was about before he found Denis on his doorstep, ready to knock again.

"Where is the attack?" He grabbed his bag and followed Denis out to the barn.

"The university. I told you we should never have left." Denis shot him a look.

Conall climbed up onto Aengus's back. "I had to help my dad with the harvest. You know that. Besides, I knew you'd come and get me as soon as the attacks started up again."

"Never mind the eight-hour ride." Denis shook his head and urged his horse on.

Conall chuckled and caught up. He hadn't wanted to leave Cork, but when the attacks had stopped, he figured Leana had moved on. It made his heart heavy, knowing he'd missed her again, but he'd taken the chance to return home. He would catch up to her eventually. He always did.

Conall stood at the door of the dorm, bracing himself. Shouts had erupted a few moments before, which meant that whatever had been attacking was still inside. He shoved the door open, lowering his crossbow to take aim at whatever had caused the uproar. His heart leapt into his throat.

Leana dropped the young man's hand and jumped away. Her beauty drew Conall in like it had countless times before—even after all these months. Her mouth dropped open when she saw who it was. "Conall."

He should end this right then and there. One bolt and she would be gone. Instead, he held his finger up to his lips and moved further into the room. "Go. Now. Others will be here at any moment, and I won't be able to stop them. I'll meet you where we had dinner on the coast. Go."

Pain filled her eyes as she stared at him for a second more, then disappeared out the window. Conall had wanted to be wrong. While he'd suspected her for months, he had never had concrete evidence until that moment. He'd hoped she would just fade into the background so he wouldn't have to hunt her like so many other creatures before her. But then she had gotten too careless, leading every hunter in Ireland to her trail.

And he'd let her go.

Voices filled the hallway as the others ran into the room.

"It's too late. She's gone." Conall stared at the window, ignoring the student who lay still in his bed.

"What happened? You should have been in there in time." Denis glared at him.

Conall sighed. "I suspect the victim was dead within seconds after the yelling began."

Denis moved into the room and searched through the papers. "No music. No art. Sounds like we have the right creature. Did you at least catch what she looked like?"

Beautiful. Eyes that pulled you in. Hair that he longed to run his fingers through. Conall shook his head. "She's too good. But we know she has to be around here somewhere. We'll probably have to set some guards in every dorm until she's caught." Conall glanced down at the young man and frowned as he left. Such potential. Gone too soon at the hands of the woman he loved.

Leana stood not far from where Conall had found her nearly a year before. She looked exactly the same if not more beautiful as she stared out at the ocean. She turned when she heard him approach, her eyes guarded.

"You're a hunter?" Her voice was flat.

"Yes. And you're Leanan Sidhe." He didn't mean the accusatory tone, but even after he'd witnessed it himself, he hadn't wanted to admit it.

Her eyes registered surprise. "How——?"

"I've hunted long enough to know all of the creatures in this land. But you were the hardest to track down. And believe me, I wanted to be wrong." He brushed a strand of hair from her face.

She nodded. "I'd hoped I could draw the scent off me, but I guess I messed up, didn't I?"

"So it was you who set the vampire free?" Anger burned, but he pushed it down. No wonder she'd wanted him away from the case. She knew how dangerous Dearg Due was. "I guess I should have suspected."

"You are the first human who has not succumbed to me." She turned and faced him. "And you're the first human I couldn't bring myself to end."

Conall laughed and took her hands in his. "I guess we've both failed at our destinies. You're the first demon I've come across that I couldn't end."

Leana wrapped her arms around his neck, searching his eyes. "I've said it before, and I have to repeat it again. We can't be together. I would kill you just by loving you."

"That's where I believe you're wrong." He leaned down and kissed her. "We've shared parts of your soul, and I think we could do it again."

She cocked her head to the side. "But then . . ."

"Then I would become like you."

Leana shook her head. "That's not possible. It has never been done before."

Conall let go of her and pulled out his notes. "Listen, I've hunted dark creatures since I was a child. I know how most of them work. I know what kills them and what makes them stronger. Being away from you for all of these months has given me time to think. I believe that if we . . . share each other's soul, we can live off each other and avoid killing others."

Leana's eyes widened. "Conall, I—"

"Do you want to be with me?" He searched her eyes. He'd met the eyes of many dark creatures over the years, and this was the first time he saw human emotions war within them. Love, worry, fear. Things that no demon should feel, but somewhere along the way, he'd helped awaken those in her.

"How do we know this will work?" Her lip trembled. "I have only heard of one being as dangerous as the Leanan Sidhe, and he has not been seen for decades, if not centuries."

"I'm done running from you." He smiled and pulled out a ring made of iron. "It's because of my great-great-grandfather that Gancanagh no longer roams the earth. It's only fitting that I take Gancanagh's place. But if this doesn't work and I die, wear this, and you'll come with me to the land of the dead. Either way, we'll be together."

Leana stared at the ring in horror. Conall had learned that iron was the one thing her kind feared, the one thing that could kill them. Leana pulled out a pouch and held it open so that Conall could drop the ring inside. "What do we have to do?"

EPILOGUE

LEANA

Leana stood on the outskirts of the crowd, listening as the symphony on the stage played a haunting, yet beautiful piece. She rubbed her belly, proud of the small bump that was beginning to form. The new Leanan Sidhe would be born soon, leaving Leana to roam the earth with Conall.

She looked over as Conall made his way around the people. His eyes danced as he came near. She nodded toward the stage. "You did well."

"Isn't the melody beautiful? I knew it was something the world needed to hear as soon as I came across the composer." Conall beamed. This had been his first time as Gancanagh to inspire a musician. He was careful not to kill, though it had taken a few tries on his part. Instead of sucking them dry, both he and Leana only took what was needed to survive, sharing the spirits between the two of them. He bent down and kissed her. "Ready to go? Da will be expecting us soon for dinner."

"Yes, I was just waiting for you." Leana moved away from the crowd and smiled as Conall put his arm around her, holding her close. She'd been the Leanan Sidhe for centuries, created countless pieces of art, and stolen countless souls. It was time to move on to the next grand adventure with the man she loved by her side.

ABOUT THE AUTHOR

Jaclyn is an Idaho farm girl who grew up loving to read. She developed a love for writing at a young age and published her first book in 2013. She met her husband, Steve, at BYU, and they have six happy, crazy children who encourage her to keep writing. After owning a bookstore and running away to have adventures in Australia, they settled back down in their home in Utah. Jaclyn now spends her days herding her kids to various activities and trying to remember what she was supposed to do next. Her books include the Lost in a Fairy Tale Series ~ Endless, Timeless, Fearless, and Limitless; Magicians of the Deep; Leana; Keela; and the Luck series, which helped feed her obsession with all things Irish. You can learn more about her at www.jaclynweist.com

.

More From Jaclyn Weist

<u>Lost in a Fairy Tale</u>
Timeless
Fearless
Endless
Limitless

<u>The Luck Series</u>
Stolen Luck
Twist of Luck
Best of Luck
More Than Just Luck
No Such Luck
Just My Luck

<u>The Lost Luck Series</u>
Seeking His Luck
Pushing His Luck
Finding His Luck

<u>The Gates of Atlantis</u>
Magicians of the Deep

<u>Celtic Fairy Tale Romances</u>
Leana
Keela